"Your mother and I want to go for a ride. Will you ride with me on Blackie? I promise you'll be safe."

"Where will I sit?"

"Right in front of me."

It took at least a half a minute before he said, "Okay."

Victory! A small one, but a victory nevertheless. They were making progress.

After Holden's gaze connected with Jessica's, he got out of the truck and opened the trailer for her while he went in the barn for Blackie. Chase stayed by her as he brought his horse out.

"He's huge!"

"He needs to be in order to hold both of us." Holden mounted him. "Come on up."

Before Chase could make up his mind, Holden caught him and helped him settle in. "See how easy that was? You just lean back against me and we'll start walking. You can't fall because I've got you."

Dear Reader,

The idea for *Home on the Ranch: Wyoming Sheriff* came to me in the most unexpected way. One of my married sons is a master mechanic. He told me he'd just escaped a harrowing situation. It seems a truck that he'd put on a hoist so he could work underneath it literally broke in half. The whole back end crashed to the cement where he'd been standing only seconds before. Clearly he would have been killed. An investigation discovered that the owner had loaded the bed too heavily and the frame wasn't built to handle the weight. I shivered over that accident.

It got me thinking about the safety of the world of the mechanic. The trust between him and the client is imperative. But what if one or the other has evil intentions? Before I knew it, I'd come up with a story about a widow who is investigating the death of her mechanic husband. You'll have to read what happens when she seeks out the sheriff.

Enjoy!

Rebecca Winters

HOME *on the* RANCH

WYOMING
SHERIFF

— ⚒ —

REBECCA
WINTERS

H™ **HARLEQUIN**® HOME ON THE RANCH

Recycling programs
for this product may
not exist in your area.

ISBN-13: 978-1-335-47487-2

Home on the Ranch: Wyoming Sheriff

Copyright © 2019 by Rebecca Winters

Printed in U.S.A.

www.Harlequin.com

Rebecca Winters, whose family of four children has now swelled to include five beautiful grandchildren, lives in Salt Lake City, Utah, in the land of the Rocky Mountains. Living near canyons and high alpine meadows full of wildflowers, she never runs out of places to explore. They, plus her favorite vacation spots in Europe, often end up as backgrounds for her romance novels, because writing is her passion, along with her family and church.

Rebecca loves to hear from readers. If you wish to email her, please visit her website, cleanromances.net.

Books by Rebecca Winters

Harlequin Western Romance

Wind River Cowboys

The Right Cowboy
Stranded with the Rancher

Sapphire Mountain Cowboys

A Valentine for the Cowboy
Made for the Rancher
Cowboy Doctor
Roping Her Christmas Cowboy

Lone Star Lawmen

The Texas Ranger's Bride
The Texas Ranger's Nanny
The Texas Ranger's Family
Her Texas Ranger Hero

Visit the Author Profile page
at Harlequin.com for more titles.

To my brilliant, wonderful, third-born son, who brings joy to the lives of our family with his happy disposition and can put a car back together better than anyone you've ever seen. Ask his wife, who never worries about them getting stranded in their Jeep in the backcountry of Moab, Utah. She knows he's a genius who will always bring them home.

Chapter 1

The beautiful Thursday morning beckoned to Jessica Fleming. She walked out the back of the ranch house to the barn with more energy than usual. After deciding to ride bareback, she took her deceased husband's buckskin for a ride around the fenced-in pasture while her five-year-old son watched. Her own horse she'd had to put down a year ago because of illness.

"Bucky is frisky today, Mom!"

"He sure is. It must be the effect of the sun after yesterday's rainstorm. I bet he's hungry. Would you like to help me feed him?"

"No. I'll put water in the bucket." He'd taken on that job in addition to filling the hay net in the barn. She left the door open. That way Bucky could come and go from the pasture at will.

Chase's answer was always the same and discouraged her. He was afraid of horses. Not even her husband, Trent, who'd once been a terrific bull rider, could get him to ride on one. Neither of them could understand his fear, but there it was.

Since her husband's death two years ago, she'd ridden or exercised Bucky every day in the morning. Chase usually played near the barn.

At Christmas she'd bought Chase a Big League Blaster Gun because he'd begged for it. It had come with twelve foam darts. He'd lost three of them and could shoot it only out here using the fencing for a target. Secretly she'd be glad when he'd lost all the darts.

After a good run, she dismounted. "See you tonight, Bucky."

She patted his rump and called to Chase. "Want to come and help me clean the garage?"

"I bet there's a lot of good stuff!"

"I *know* there is." It was all getting thrown out.

They worked until lunch, then she drove her son to afternoon kindergarten at Gannett Peak Elementary School in the town of Whitebark, Wyoming.

"See you later, honey." Once she saw him run onto the playground with the other kids, she returned to the ranch house to finish working on the garage. With summer almost here, she had to make room for Chase's bike and plastic swimming pool, among other things. She also needed to buy a new car badly and had decided to get a Toyota.

Memorial Day would be on Monday and school would be out for the summer, making it a long weekend. Today was Thursday, her day off from the hair salon her mother owned. Jessica needed to make the most of her free time. Once she'd loaded the boxes of things she'd gone through to discard and take to the dump, she should be back in time to pick up Chase from school.

After Trent's death, the two-car garage had become a storeroom that needed to be cleaned out completely. Jessica could hardly park their truck inside.

In the beginning she hadn't been able to throw anything away because most of it had belonged to her mechanic husband. But now it had to be done. Already she'd had a garage sale and had sold his ski equipment, snowshoes and trail bike.

The big items like the truck and Trent's tools needed to go next. She'd driven over to the auto dealership yesterday where he'd started working soon after graduating from high school. A couple of the guys like Bryan and Eddie who'd been his friends had shown interest in buying both, but were too busy to make an offer right then. She said she'd be back.

Jessica had taken Chase with her. He loved to watch what went on at the shop. Everyone there made a fuss over him that warmed her heart. When her son was born, his hair had come in a light blond like Jessica's. But in time it had turned dark blond like his dad's.

Chase had also inherited his father's lean build and happy smile. All the guys commented on the resemblance. Jessica had hoped to get pregnant again soon so he'd have a brother or sister, but it didn't happen. After undergoing several tests, she'd learned her body was going through early menopause and she'd never conceive again. That was a revelation she was still dealing with and had made their son Chase a thousand times more precious to both of them.

Remembering her husband caused her to take an extra breath. *Keep working, Jessica.*

Almost done, she backed up the truck and started loading the last few boxes she'd gone through onto the bed. She couldn't wait to get busy with the broom. As she looked around, she saw one more carton in the corner partially hidden by the lawn mower and walked over to get it. If it held Christmas decorations, it was in the wrong place. Curious to see what was inside, Jessica opened it.

A gasp escaped her lips when she saw four ball joints. She let go of the box and jumped to her feet as if she'd been burned.

Two years ago Trent had been test-driving her car in the rain in the early hours of the morning and had gone off the road into a ditch. The car had turned over on top of him and he'd been killed. Chase was the only reason she'd managed to get through her grief.

The police investigation had determined that a loose ball joint had been the reason for the accident. The whole wheel had fallen off because the tie rod, steering rod and the axle had snapped, as well.

When she'd told Trent her car was having problems, he'd gone out to take a look. After checking it, he told her he was going to replace all four ball joints to keep her safe and would do it after work. Around seven that evening she drove the truck to the dealership with Chase to take her husband a hamburger and fries for dinner while he worked.

They waited for Trent, who finally lowered the car from the lift and drove it out to the enclosed parking area. He was going to leave it there overnight and take it for a test run in the morning. She remembered him putting some things in the back of the truck before he closed up and they went home.

Was *this* the box he'd brought with them that night along with his tools?

She knelt down and examined the ball joints. All four were worn and loose. These *had* to be the ones he'd taken off her car. There'd be no reason for them to be in the garage otherwise. It meant he'd used the four *new* ball joints from this box he'd purchased from the dealership's parts department to put on her car.

But if Trent had installed all four new ones, why did the police say that her car had a loose ball joint and it had caused the fatal crash that had left her traumatized, and Chase without a father? It didn't make sense when she was staring at the four worn ones he'd removed. Or had this box been sitting in the garage a lot longer than two years ago…?

While she was trying to figure it out, a feeling of unease enveloped her. She knew something wasn't right. By this time it was getting too late to go to the dump, but it didn't matter. She left the box in the garage.

After closing the tailgate, she climbed in the truck and used the remote to close the garage door before she took off. Once she'd picked up Chase from school, she drove to Style Clips. All the way there, her heart pounded unmercifully with her thoughts growing darker by the second.

She gave her mom a quick phone call to let her know that she was coming. After letting herself in the back door of the four-chair shop with her key, she unlocked another door and hurried up the stairs to the apartment above. Chase led the way.

"Nana?"

"Mom?"

"Well, hi!" A smile broke out on her mother's face. She'd just turned fifty-two, but didn't look it. "Don't those new jeans and emoji shirt look adorable on you!"

"Hi, Nana!" Chase's brown eyes lit up and he ran to her.

She gave him a kiss. "Come in the kitchen and tell me about school. I just made some doughnuts for the party at the church on Saturday. Ray's taking me. But you can put some sprinkles on top of the icing and have one."

"Yum!"

Jessica went to the fridge to pour him a glass of milk, then put the carton away. Chase scrambled over to the kitchen table where a batch of doughnuts was waiting for toppings. Her mother put one on a plate for him, then walked over to the counter. She shot her a glance out of eyes as green as Jessica's.

"What's going on?" she asked in a low voice. "I thought this was your day to finish cleaning the garage and didn't expect to see you. I can tell something's wrong."

"It's about Trent's accident."

Her mother frowned. "What do you mean?"

While Chase was still occupied, Jessica told her about the box of four worn ball joints she'd found in a corner of the garage.

"The night before the accident, I was there in the bay when Trent changed all of them and drove my car out to the lot for the night. He'd said he would take a test run in the morning like he always did.

"As you know, I watched him finish up. If he hadn't done the whole job, he would have told me. But the police said it was a loose ball joint that caused the car to overturn. When I questioned the investigating officer about what they'd found, he said I must have misunderstood because Trent obviously hadn't changed all of them.

"I was so devastated he'd been killed, I wasn't thinking clearly and decided that had to have been the case. For two years I haven't thought about it. But just now I found a box with four worn, loose ball joints. Those have to be the ones he took off and brought home. So how do you explain that?"

"I don't know, honey. For one thing, why didn't he just throw them away at work?"

"Trent often brought stuff home with the idea of using it. In fact, you should see the boxes of junk I'm taking to the dump."

Her mother's happy expression had turned to one of alarm. "Have you told anyone else about this?" she asked in a quiet voice.

"No. I came straight here."

"Where's the box?"

"I left it in the garage. Mom—I don't like what I'm thinking."

"You're not the only one. You need to go to the police and talk to the investigating officer."

"I don't remember who it was."

"Ask to speak to the police chief first."

"I will, but I'm doing a color on Rachel Bates in the morning. Her appointments are set in stone. Following her, Seth Lunt will be in for a haircut." She'd appreciated that three of the guys from the dealership had come in from time to time for a trim, but only Seth came anymore.

Lines had marred her mother's features. "I'll take over for you. Tell the chief what you've discovered. Show him the box. I'd like an explanation myself. Bring Chase over here on your way. I'll put him to work sweeping the floor of the shop until you get back. He loves that job."

"You think there's something wrong, too."

"Yes, however I suppose there could be a logical explanation we haven't thought of."

Jessica nodded. "Maybe Trent decided not to replace one of them after all, but then why would he say that he did?"

Her mom looked as perplexed as she felt. "Did you actually watch him replace every one of them?"

"No. I was watching Chase and he kept wanting to run around. But we were right there the whole time. I'm just not sure of anything now. What if someone tampered with my car after Trent put it out in the lot?"

They stared at each other as unspoken messages flashed between them. "You need to look into it immediately."

"I agree." Out of earshot of Chase, she called the police station and asked to speak to the police chief to make an appointment.

"Sorry. Sheriff Granger won't be back until Tuesday. Come in to the station then."

"All right. Thank you." She hung up disappointed, but there wasn't anything else to do. She turned to her mother and hugged her hard. "The sheriff won't be in until Tuesday so I'll have to wait. Thank you for encouraging me and letting me know I'm not crazy. Thank you for everything. I love you."

The first year after Trent's death had come close to

destroying her. She had adored her husband and her anguish over knowing she could never have another baby made her feel as if she'd suffered two deaths. Her specialist did say that in some cases, an early menopause diagnosis didn't mean *never.* Conception could happen, but it was in the almost miraculous category.

This last year had been a little better and Chase was her everything. She was starting to see light at the end of the tunnel, but the sight of those ball joints had thrown her back to the past in a horrible way.

"Mom?" came her son's voice.

She turned to him. His mouth was covered in icing and sprinkles. "I sprinkled some doughnuts for you and Nana."

"Thank you, darling."

Early Friday morning, Riverside Cemetery in Cody, Wyoming, was already filling with flowers for Memorial Day on Monday, but the main press of visitors wouldn't be felt until the actual day.

Thirty-year-old Holden Granger had been vacationing in Cody with his parents and siblings for the last week. He'd been born and raised here where he'd imagined living for the rest of his life. But when his wife, Cynthia, had died of lymphoma three years ago, his entire world had changed forever.

He'd come to the cemetery at ten to place a potted red rose tree on Cynthia's grave beneath the headstone.

Beloved Wife.
Death leaves a heartache no one can heal.
Love leaves a memory no one can steal.

After burying her, his pain had been so great, he couldn't imagine being alive another day. Yet after this long without her, he'd learned that time was helping him to move on.

The town of Cody represented the past and his work as a police officer. This was where he'd met Cynthia and would always treasure the memories of her. But to his surprise he found himself actually looking forward to the drive back to Whitebark, Wyoming, where he now lived. Until Tuesday he would follow up on some chores he'd been putting off.

He thought back to the six months after her death. His police chief had suggested he apply for the police chief job in Whitebark. The chief thought a change of location might help him throw off his depression. Holden looked into it and learned that the Whitebark chief had resigned because of bad health. There was a vacancy and Holden had the credentials they were looking for. Once hired, he'd sold the house and relocated. Though he missed his family, he hadn't been sorry or looked back.

Holden kissed two fingers and pressed them to the top of the granite headstone before walking to his dark blue Subaru Outback under a semicloudy sky. He'd been away from work a week and wondered what messes had piled up in his absence.

Having said his goodbyes last night to the family that included two married sisters and brothers-in-law, plus a niece and nephew, he took off for his five-hour drive back to the Wind River Mountains.

Holden had never thought he could love that range as much as the Absarokas outside Cody. How wrong he'd been once the friends he'd made in the Whitebark fire department took him camping and introduced him to some of their favorite spots!

For the first time in a week he turned on the radio to listen to the Hunt Talk call-in show covering the western half of the state.

After two stops in Thermopolis and Lander for food, he reached Whitebark at five in the afternoon. Before going to his ranch, he pulled into the back of the Sublette County sheriff's office near the county courthouse. Walt Emerson had been acting as undersheriff while Granger had been out of town.

In an election held several months after Holden had been made police chief, he'd been voted in as sheriff to replace the one who'd passed away unexpectedly. He'd inherited a department that covered the whole county where he maintained a staff of thirty-four sworn officers.

The extra responsibility kept him so busy he didn't have much time to think about the absence of a special woman in his life. He dated on occasion, but none of the relationships had grown serious.

Holden entered the building through the back door. He waved to Jenny in the dispatch room, then walked down the hall to his office. Walt sat at the desk in front of the computer. The forty-five-year-old man looked up. "Hey—are you ever a sight for sore eyes!"

"What's the matter?"

"You might as well ask me what *isn't* wrong!"

Holden grinned. "I believe you're on duty until I come in on Tuesday morning."

"Don't remind me. Thank heaven you're back in case an emergency comes up I can't solve."

"That'll be the day. I thought I'd see how things are

going before I head to my ranch and work on some projects I've been putting off since I moved here."

"Just don't forget the new members of TTSAR will be meeting with you on Tuesday morning." The Tip Top Search and Rescue volunteer unit for the county needed staffing from time to time. "You'll also need to choose the new engraver for the Ranch Watch program."

"I tapped Rex Lewis for that job two weeks ago." To pinpoint the ranches and farms from where machinery was stolen, the owners' names were engraved on it to identify specific locations of theft.

"Three days ago Rex fell off a ladder fixing his barn roof and broke his elbow."

Holden shook his head. Great. "Okay, I'll check in on him." He sorted through the paperwork in the inbox on the desk.

"Also, just so you know, the detention center is at capacity. We can't handle any more than fifty inmates."

"I'll phone Rand over at the marshal's office to figure it out. Anything else?"

Walt frowned. "Jan Allred's son Mike has been on a hunger strike. His mother is frantic and has called here three times looking for you. You remember she works in the bakery at Loft's supermarket."

He nodded. "On Tuesday I'll have a talk with Lieutenant Fogarty over at the jail. After he gives me his view of the situation, I'll get in touch with her. Is that everything?"

The older man laughed. "Are you sure you want to know?"

"Maybe not."

"How was your vacation?"

"Good. I helped my dad do a lot of fencing."

"In other words, you're ready for a real vacation."

To his mind, a real vacation included being with his wife, but that wasn't possible and hadn't been for three years. "It was great to see my folks and family, but honestly I'm glad to be back." He was grateful to have a reason to get up every morning, including exercising his horse.

"Then go on home and enjoy your last few days of freedom."

"Thanks, Walt."

Holden left the office, nodded to the staff on duty and left for his ranch. Before moving here he'd bought the place close to the south end of town with a house and barn. After trailing his horse to Whitebark, he'd intended to put in crops of alfalfa and hay, maybe even some cattle one day. So far he'd done none of it. His life was too crazy to be the rancher he'd assumed he'd be. Maybe when he retired…

While he'd been gone this last week, Drake Simpson, the nineteen-year-old son of Hank and Allie Simpson, his neighbors to the south, took care of Blackie. The Simpsons ran a small miniature horse farm on their ranch. Drake usually came by five times a week to feed and exercise his horse, depending on Holden's schedule.

All looked well as he checked on his gelding before going in the house. No sooner had he entered the front door than his cell rang. He checked the caller ID and smiled to see his friend's name. Porter Ewing worked for the forest service after transferring in from the Adirondacks. He was a part-time firefighter and like Holden, he was single.

He clicked On. "Hey, Porter—what's up?"

"We just pulled into the station after coming back from a fire over at Roper's Discount Mattress. Cole and I saw your Subaru headed for the office. Welcome back!"

"It's good to be home. How's it going?"

"Don't ask. Want to grab a bite at Angelino's later? Wyatt will be coming with a couple of the guys."

"Sounds great. Give me an hour and I'll meet you there."

"You're on! See you soon."

On Memorial Day morning, Jessica reached for her cell phone to call her mother. "Hi, Mom."

"Hi, honey. Are you ready?"

"We are. I want to know how the church party went on Saturday night. Did you go with Ray?"

"It was fun. I had a nice time with him."

"Good." Ray Marsden was a widower who went to their church. Jessica had a feeling he was interested in her mom. "On my way over to the shop, I'm planning to buy some flowers at the florist to put on all the graves."

"Thank you for doing that. By the time you get here, I'll be ready. I've been packing us a picnic to enjoy while we're over there."

"Great. I'll be on my way as soon as I take care of Bucky."

Later, when she parked the truck behind a row of cars at the cemetery, crowds of people were already visiting the graves and it made their progress slow. She carried the box of potted flowers. Her mom trailed behind with the picnic basket.

Chase looked up at her. "How come you bought so many plants, Mom?"

"Because we have to decorate my grandparents' grave, plus the graves of your father's parents and uncle and aunt."

"And Dad's!"

"His most of all, darling."

They reached the first set of graves where Trent's family was buried. She put the box down. "I bought yellow, lavender and white mums. Choose which ones you want to put on the two headstones."

Her son pulled out the lavender potted flowers and carefully placed them at the base of each.

"That's perfect, Chase! Now let's go to my grandparents' graves." She picked up the box and they walked the short distance. "Do you know who they are?"

"Yup! My great-grandparents."

She put down the box to hug him. "That's right. They're the Harrisons and have just one headstone."

"Can I put yellow flowers on their grave, Nana?"

"I wish you would. Yellow was my mother's favorite color. Go ahead and do it."

He reached in the box and walked it over to the headstone. Jessica shared a soulful glance with her mother. Chase was so adorable. After he placed a pot of flowers, he came running to her. "Now can we go to Daddy's grave?"

She'd been waiting for him to ask. "Yes."

They walked the short distance. "I saved the white flowers for him."

"Is that your favorite color, darling?"

"Yes. My teacher at Sunday school says everyone in heaven wears white."

With that comment, tears pricked Jessica's eyes. "She's right."

"There's Daddy's grave!" He pulled out the last of the potted flowers and put them at the base of his father's headstone. Maybe Trent was watching. Jessica hoped so. Then Chase did something that surprised her and sat down on the grass next to it. "Can we have our picnic right here?"

"Of course we can," her mother answered for her and sat down by him.

Jessica pulled out her phone and took a picture. Then she, too, sank down under the sunny sky and they ate the fried chicken and potato salad.

"Mmm. This is good, Nana."

"It was your father's favorite meal when he came to my house with your mom."

After a moment of silence, Chase said, "I wish my daddy didn't have to die." His brown eyes had teared up.

"I know how you feel," Jessica murmured. "My daddy died when I was twelve. We'll always miss them, won't we?"

He nodded his dark blond head. "Where's his grave?"

"In Riverside, California, with his parents'. That's why Nana and I fly there every year and put flowers on their graves."

"Oh." Chase finished a roll and got to his feet. "Can I go look around at the flags?"

"For a few minutes, but don't go far."

"I won't." He walked off. Jessica kept her eyes on him.

Tuesday was finally here. Jessica hadn't slept well and was anxious to talk to the sheriff. She exercised

Bucky, then showered and washed her hair. With the help of the dryer and brush, she styled her blond hair into a neck-length bob. After looking in the closet, she pulled out a summery skirt and blouse to put on.

With her makeup done, she fed Chase and took him to her mom's. She'd packed his lunch and his favorite bag of building blocks. When she got there, Millie, one of the hairdressers, was already at work washing Lily Owens's hair. The beautiful onetime Olympic alpine skier was working with her parents breeding horses these days.

They all chatted for a minute. After going upstairs with Chase, she promised him she'd be back soon to take him home. Then she left the salon and headed for the complex to the sheriff's office. Once she'd parked at the rear of the building, she entered and spoke to a Deputy Sykes at the front desk.

"I was told to come in so I could speak to Chief Granger."

"Just a moment."

While she waited, she asked him if he could look up her husband's case in the files and find out the name of the investigating officer.

She had to wait a half hour before she was told the officer had retired and moved out of state. She would have to take up the matter with the chief.

To her relief, she didn't have to wait long before he said, "Mrs. Fleming? I checked with the sheriff. He can see you in ten minutes, but it will have to be short because of his loaded schedule."

Thank goodness. "I appreciate him fitting me in at all."

"Wait here. I'll let you know when you can go in."

The more Jessica thought about what she'd discovered, the more she was convinced a crime had been committed. But against whom? Her or Trent? Or was it sheer vandalism?

"Mrs. Fleming?" Jessica jumped. She'd been so deep in thought, she hadn't been aware of time passing. "You can go in now. It's the door at the end of the hall on the right around the corner."

"Thank you, Deputy."

The busy office hummed with activity. She walked down the hall and knocked on the door.

"Come in," sounded a deep male voice.

When she opened the door, her gaze traveled to the brown-haired sheriff who stood up and walked around his desk to shake her hand. She felt the warmth of it permeate her insides. He was probably in his early thirties.

Not only was he tall and well built, he was one of the most ruggedly handsome men she'd ever seen in her life. After she'd met and fallen in love with Trent, she really hadn't noticed other men. Since his death, life had passed in a kind of dull, painful blur…until now.

"Mrs. Fleming?"

"Thank you for seeing me on such short notice, Sheriff Granger."

"I'm happy to do it. Please, sit down."

She sat on one of the chairs near his desk before he took his place behind it. Like the deputies she'd seen in the building, he wore a tan shirt and black pants, nothing exceptional. But on him, they looked *good*. His silvery-gray eyes had a luminous quality that rivaled the silver badge worn on his pocket.

Though she realized he'd been the police chief at

the time of Trent's death, she'd never met him. But his name had come up in the news and during the election that had put him in as sheriff.

"Tell me what has brought you to my office."

Not wanting to waste his time, she quickly related everything she'd told her mother on Thursday. By the time she'd finished, his dark brows had formed a bar above his incredible gray eyes. He sat forward in his swivel chair.

"Was anyone else in the bay or still on the premises while you were there waiting for him?"

"I didn't see another soul."

"Okay. Where is the box of ball joints now?"

"In my garage. I was planning to take it to the dump along with some other boxes."

"Tell you what. I've got appointments all day. Why don't I come by your house this evening to have a look when it's convenient for you. I believe you mentioned you have a son."

"Yes. Chase is five and goes to kindergarten, except that he's out now for the summer."

He smiled, turning her heart over. What on earth was the matter with her? "That's a great age. When does he go to bed?"

"Seven thirty."

"Then if it's all right with you, I'll drop by about quarter to eight. Give me your phone number and I'll text you when I arrive so I won't wake him. I have a lot of questions," he explained, "and we'll be able to talk at length."

Surprised at his thoughtfulness and willingness to act so quickly, she obliged him. "You don't know what this means to me. Thank you so much." She got up from the chair. "Last night I couldn't sleep. If someone tampered with the car during that night and I can prove it, then I can't help but wonder if the culprit had wanted to injure Trent...or if I was the target, assuming that person knew it was my car."

The sheriff got to his feet and walked her to the door. "It's too soon to know anything yet, Mrs. Fleming, but I'll get back to you."

"Thank you so much, Sheriff."

Chapter 2

Holden was aware of a flowery fragrance emanating from her before he shut the door. How could he have lived in the small town of Whitebark for the last two and a half years and never have met her until now? In all honesty Holden had been totally unprepared for the sight of the beautiful blond widow with eyes the color of green diamonds.

Almost as shocking was what she'd told him about the box she'd found Thursday in her garage and what it could mean. He'd been working in law enforcement since college and had learned never to discount a victim's story until he'd carried out a full investigation.

Because Holden had been the police chief at the time of her husband's accident, Mrs. Fleming's reason for coming to his office with such compelling, unexpected information could have knocked him over.

He phoned Gil Manos in the back room and asked him to pull all the information on the case of Trent Fleming who'd died in an automobile accident two years ago. If there was anything in the evidence room, he wanted to see it.

For the rest of the day he put out fires and found himself looking at his watch. At six o'clock, Gil brought a file to his desk and a shoebox. Inside was the ball joint from the car that had been totaled. Holden was surprised and pleased it had still been in the room. Every year the place was gone through and normally unnecessary evidence of this type was tossed.

With everything he needed, he drove home in his police truck labeled Sheriff. He ate a sandwich and read through the file about the tragic accident before heading for the Fleming ranch on East Ash Road. After he pulled into her driveway, he texted Jessica that he was in front.

She texted back that she would open the garage door so he could see the contents of the box first. In another minute the door lifted. He got out of the truck to join her, carrying the shoebox.

This evening she'd dressed in jeans and a blue top. After seeing her earlier, he realized her attractive figure would stand out in anything she wore. He felt her eyes on him as he walked up to her.

"Good evening, Mrs. Fleming. I take it your son is in bed." He put the shoebox on the cement.

"And hopefully asleep. Thank you for coming. This is the box."

He hunkered down and opened it. Inside were four worn ball joints. As he took the lid off the shoebox, he heard her slight gasp. "I—Is that the ball joint that caused the accident?" she stammered.

The tremor in her voice tugged at his emotions. Holden knew more than anyone what it was like to be reminded of the spouse you'd loved and lost.

"Yes. It was still in the evidence room. If you don't mind, I'm going to put everything in my truck and take it to forensics in the morning for testing. Then I'll come in the house so I can ask you some questions."

"I'll open the front door for you."

"Tell me something. Did you buy your Dodge Charger new or used?"

"New. It had 120,000 miles on it when Trent decided to replace the ball joints."

"That's important to know. I'll be right back."

He put the boxes on the rear seat and returned to the house. She led him through the foyer to the living room with its traditional decor. Holden admired the framed photographs of The Winds and several still-life paintings hanging on the walls.

On the end tables and mantel over the fireplace were photos of her son and family. Her home had charm and warmth. There was nothing like a woman's touch. When he'd moved here, he hadn't had Cynthia who would have made his new house into their home.

"Please sit down. Can I offer you something to drink? Coffee or tea? Or maybe a soda?"

"Nothing, thank you." He chose one of the upholstered chairs.

"All right." She sank down on the end of the couch.

"If I find a criminal act has been committed, then I'll conduct a full investigation. For now it's important

I get a picture of your life and relatives, the friends you see."

"I understand."

He pulled his digital recorder out of his shirt pocket and placed it on the coffee table. "I prefer to record the information so I don't miss anything."

She nodded.

"What's your full name and age?"

"Jessica Stevens Fleming. I'm almost twenty-seven."

"Where were you born? Give me some details about your family."

"Riverside, California, where my father Wayne Stevens was born. He was a former bull rider in the rodeo. Later he did stunt work for the movies, but he was killed when I was twelve. My mother, Erica Harrison, was born here in Whitebark, but went to college in California. She met my father at the rodeo.

"They married fast and she became a cosmetologist to help support them. After his death, we moved here to be with her parents, the Harrisons, on their ranch. Since then they've both passed away and she rents the ranch to a family while she lives in town over the beauty shop."

He nodded. "Now tell me about your husband and his family."

"Trent was born here. His parents and aunt died early in a plane accident so his Uncle Paul raised him in this house. He was a horse person and a mechanic on the side until he died. In high school, Trent did bull riding like my father, and he won some local rodeos sponsored by the Wyoming Rodeo Association before joining the Pro Rodeo Association.

"But by then Trent and I wanted to get married. His

uncle urged him to give up the rodeo and learn to be a mechanic so he could make a steady living. When his uncle died, Trent inherited this ranch and the horses."

"Did you and your husband ride?"

"Yes. I'm trying to get Chase interested, but so far he's afraid."

"I bet he gets over that in time." Holden looked around. "You've created a lovely home. I especially like the pictures of the mountains. They're spectacular. Who's the photographer?"

"I am. I like to dabble."

"I'm impressed."

"Thank you."

"How did you and your husband meet?"

"We both went to Whitebark High School and started dating when we were sophomores." A quick, lovely smile appeared. "That proved to be it for both of us."

Holden could relate. He and Cynthia had met in high school, too.

"My mother started working at Style Clips after we moved here. Eventually she bought it from the owner and pushed me to get my cosmetology certificate, which I did. I wanted to be an elementary school teacher, but my college plans changed when Trent and I married.

"He got a job at the Mid-Valley dealership and started commuting to Riverton to take classes for a couple of years to get his master's mechanic degree. Pretty soon we were expecting a baby. I can't think of anything else."

"You've given me excellent information," Holden interjected. "Tell me about your friends after you were married, the people with whom you associated, so I can get an idea of your life as a couple."

"Millie Edwards and Dottie Marsden, who are both married, work at the salon part-time. I'm friends with them. And I've stayed close to a couple of my school friends, especially Donna Sills who lives here and is married with two children.

"As for Trent, he had his buddies in the rodeo. After we married, he also became friends with the guys at the shop, but we didn't go out much because of his long hours."

"Tell me about his coworkers. This is especially important."

Jessica went through the list with him, starting with the owner of the dealership.

"When Trent started, there were seven full-time mechanics, the parts guys, two service writers and the receptionist. But since then I'm sure there've been changes. The employees I've known have been great to me and Chase. In the beginning they would come over to the house and bring him little gifts."

"Are all the employees from Whitebark?"

She shook her head. "As far as I know I think most of them have moved here from somewhere else."

Holden turned off the recorder and put it back in his pocket. "You've given me enough material to paint a picture. After the forensics lab has gotten back to me, I'll contact you and ask for more details. Until then, don't tell anyone anything." He got to his feet.

"I won't." She followed him to the front door. "Do you have any kind of a hunch about this?" Her eyes beseeched him.

"I will have after I do some investigating and talk to forensics. Then I'll call you."

"Thank you again, Sheriff. Just being able to tell you about this has helped me settle down. This morning I didn't think I could. Good night."

"Good night."

He would have liked to stay longer and talk to her, but this had been an official call. By the time he reached the ranch, he realized this was the first time in his career he'd been tempted to break his own rule about mixing police business with pleasure.

That rule had been stressed to him by the higher-ups when he'd started out in police work years earlier. To this point, any dates he'd made with women after moving here came from meeting them socially or with friends. Mrs. Fleming was automatically on his do-not-get-involved list.

Jessica had awakened in surprisingly good spirits on Wednesday morning considering she'd asked Sheriff Granger to investigate what she'd discovered. She could see why he was the sheriff. He not only radiated total confidence, but he had an aura of calm that had put her at ease when she didn't think it was possible.

The fact that the busy head of law enforcement had come over to her house last evening after putting in a full day's work showed his determination to get to the bottom of her suspicions.

She was still thinking about him when she drove to her mom's with Chase who got busy playing with his toys.

"Tell me about the sheriff." Her mother spoke first. "Does he feel you're worrying about nothing?"

She took a deep breath. "No. Actually, I was amazed that he took what I said so seriously and acted so quickly. He brought the ball joint the police took off my car that caused Trent's accident. I couldn't believe it existed at this point, but he found it in the evidence room!"

"That *is* amazing!" Her mother shook her head. "Does he suspect tampering?"

"I think so, but he didn't say. In fact, he warned me not to say anything to anyone. He said that after he takes everything to the forensics lab and does some more investigating, he'll call me. Before he left, he turned on his recorder and interviewed me about my life."

She bit her lip. "I'm convinced he'll get to the bottom of this. He…has a way about him."

"Is he as good-looking as I remember?"

Jessica blinked. "You've seen him before?"

"He rode with the police and deputies in the Fourth of July parade last year. Remember I took Chase because you were in bed with a bad cold? I thought the sheriff looked rather handsome on his black horse."

Warmth filled Jessica's cheeks because she'd thought the same thing about him when she'd entered his office yesterday about Trent's death. In fact, it brought a guilty pang to her heart that the sheriff was even in her thoughts.

"Dottie says he's a widower. I can just imagine he has a lot of women after him."

Jessica could, too, but she wanted to change the subject. "Let me check on Chase."

"I'll go into the bedroom with you. I've got a present for him." In a minute she went to the closet and brought out a new fourteen-wheeler truck that had a little plastic driver for Chase to play with. Then the phone rang.

"I'll be right back." But when she left the room to answer the phone, he didn't go near it.

"Wow! I didn't know Nana bought you this truck."

"She didn't! Seth brought it when he came in for his haircut yesterday."

"I didn't know that."

Chase wouldn't look at her. "I heard Seth say he might buy Daddy's truck. Are you going to sell it to him?" He sounded unhappy about it.

"I have no idea."

"I don't want you to."

Her son was having a hard time letting go of Trent's memory. She knew she never would.

"When are we going to get a new car?" he asked.

"Just as soon as our truck is sold."

Chase stayed next to Jessica. She didn't understand. "What's wrong, honey?"

"I don't know."

"Is it because I'm selling it?"

His eyes filled with tears. "I wish Daddy hadn't died."

"So do I, darling. Still, I hope you thanked Seth for the gift."

He nodded. "After he gave it to me, he left because you weren't here. He asked me where you were."

She frowned. "What did you tell him?"

"That you were doing errands."

Thank goodness she hadn't told Chase where she'd really gone.

"He got mad."

"Seth did?"

"Yup. He told Nana he'd wait until *you* could cut his hair. I don't like him."

Oh, dear. Her son was feeling possessive of her. "Some people get used to one person doing it and don't want anyone else."

"I only like you to cut mine."

"I love doing it."

Her mother came back into the room, and Jessica turned to her. "Chase and I are going to go home and fill the little pool."

"Hooray!"

The three of them went downstairs and outside to the truck. Chase got in the back seat and fastened himself in his car seat.

"Mom," she whispered, "Chase just told me Seth bought him that truck."

"Oh, yes. I meant to tell you when the phone rang."

"He also said Seth didn't let you cut his hair."

Her mom darted her a concerned glance. "I think he was disappointed you weren't here and said he'd be back another time. If you want my opinion, he's been interested in you for a long time."

Jessica didn't want to believe it, but knew it was true and Chase had picked up on it. She and her son were a team. He didn't want another man changing that.

"To be honest, Mom, I wish he hadn't brought that gift over. It makes me more uncomfortable than I already am. When Bryan and Eddie stopped coming in for haircuts, I assumed I'd seen the last of Seth, too. I've been trying to figure out how to avoid him."

"If you're not here the next time he comes in, maybe he'll get the message."

"Maybe. He tells me he's afraid someone else will

ruin his long hair and cut it too short. He said he only trusts me."

"Do you like long hair, Mom?" Chase asked. The little monkey had been listening through the open window.

She shook her head. "Not on a man. Especially when it's down to his shoulders."

"How come?"

She shrugged. "I think it makes him look scruffy."

"I'm glad I look like my dad!" Chase exclaimed.

Jessica laughed. "So am I, sweetheart. So am I!"

Before taking a shower, a restless Holden looked through the police file on Trent Fleming and read the coroner's report.

Trapped victim bled out after glass laceration to the brachial artery in left upper arm. Pronounced dead at the accident scene.

It took only fifteen seconds to bleed out like that.

Trent Fleming's senseless death wouldn't leave him alone. He needed answers he could give Mrs. Fleming.

After phoning Drake, who would be over later to take care of Blackie, Holden put on a fresh uniform, packed a lunch and drove over to Sanchez Auto Salvage on Wednesday morning. While he waited in his truck for the gate to open, he ate two sausage biscuits and washed them down with the hot coffee he'd picked up for breakfast at Top Stop on the way.

Before long, one of the employees opened the gate and Holden drove on through to the office. He walked inside. "Marcos?"

"Hey, Holden. *Que tal?*"

"*Muy bien.* How are things with you?"

"So-so. What can I do for the sheriff?"

"I need help on a case. According to a police file I've been looking at, the car involved in the fatal car crash on May 15, two years ago, was towed here. The investigating officer was Luis Canaga."

"I remember. What happened to him?"

"He retired and moved to Colorado. Can you tell me if the white Dodge Charger has already been sold for parts?"

"Let me look it up on the computer."

This was a long shot, but Holden intended to look under every rock.

"It's still here, what's left of it. You'll find it over in lot twenty."

"Can I take a look?"

He nodded. "Come with me. I'm not busy yet."

Holden followed him through the car graveyard until they came to the demolished white car that had overturned on Trent during a rainstorm.

Marcos shot him a glance. "What exactly are you looking for?"

"Ball joints. There should be three of them, unless someone has bought them off you."

"Not four?"

"I have one of them."

"Ah. I'll take a look."

Marcos had worked as a mechanic and knew cars inside and out. He walked around to the front of the wreck. Holden took pictures with his camera. It took Marcos a minute. "Here's one."

"Is it old or new?"

He let out a whistle. "It's new. I'm surprised nobody has seen it."

"Interesting. What about the one below?"

"This is going to take work." He got down on the ground for a look. "Yup. Here's another new one."

Holden snapped more pictures. "I want to buy them both."

"I'll have to get my tools."

"Before you do that, I want you to check on the other side. There should be one more."

"I'll try. That side is pretty well smashed up."

"Do it for me. I'll make it worth your time."

"This must be important."

"You have no idea."

He waited five minutes before Marcos raised his head. "There's another one in there, but I'll need to cut through to get to it. It'll take me a little while."

"I'll wait if you have the time."

"Anything for you."

After Marcos went back to his office for some tools, Holden phoned the forensics lab. He was told that Cyril, the head expert, would be there in a half hour. Hopefully he'd have answers for him. Jessica Fleming deserved them as soon as possible.

Marcos returned and Holden took more pictures. After an hour he thanked the owner of the salvage yard. After he'd taken his fingerprints, he paid him well before driving to the forensics office with three new ball joints in a bag.

He found Cyril waiting for him.

"Holden? I heard you were coming. I've done a thorough inspection as you asked. Come with me. I have everything laid out for you." They moved to the lab. "This worn ball joint from the evidence room is a Duralast. The four worn ball joints in this box you brought in are made by McCoy."

"How do you know that without a serial number?"

"Our expert on parts can recognize the brands on sight."

"Did you get fingerprints on any of them?"

"Yes. The results are in the file I'll be faxing to you."

"Good. So what can your expert tell me about *these* three ball joints?" He handed him the bag.

"I'll be right back."

He returned a few minutes later. "These new ball joints are the Moog brand. It's interesting that this box holding the four worn ball joints has the Moog brand printed on it."

Some of the pieces of the puzzle were starting to fall into place. "I'll leave these three so you can lift any fingerprints. Let me know when I can come in. I appreciate your fast work."

He carried the box of examined evidence out to the truck and left for the office. Holden wished he were a detective again so he could spend all his time on this case. Instead, he had to work it in whenever he could, or after-hours. Those green eyes of hers begging for help wouldn't let go of him.

Chapter 3

Jessica had just gone through the ritual of putting Chase to bed Wednesday night and was in the kitchen doing the dinner dishes when her cell phone rang. It could be anyone. When she checked the caller ID, her heart pounded harder than it should have. She'd only experienced this with Trent in the early days of their romance.

She answered on the third ring. "Sheriff Granger?" Jessica knew she sounded out of breath.

"Yes. Am I calling too late?"

"Not at all." She sat down on one of the chairs at the kitchen table.

"If your son is still awake, we can talk tomorrow."

"No. After saying prayers and reading him six stories, he's finally asleep."

His deep chuckle resonated with her insides. "I went

through a lot of that on my trip to Cody last week to visit my family. I have two married sisters. One is expecting and the other has two children, Rob and Chrissy. She's Chase's age and kept me busy every night, insisting I put her to bed."

His comment put a smile on her face. "Sounds like she loves her uncle."

"I miss them."

Jessica couldn't forget he'd lost his wife. That made her feel guiltier than ever that he'd been on her mind. "It must be hard to come back to the kind of work you do. I feel guilty to have bothered you."

"I like what I do. Since my wife died of cancer three years ago, it's what keeps me going."

"I'm sorry for your loss, Sheriff." Her voice caught. "If I didn't have Chase…"

"We all need a reason to go on living."

"I agree. I'm thankful you're working on Trent's case."

"That's why I'm calling. I want to give you an update on what I've discovered so far."

"Oh, good… Are you going to tell me this has been about nothing, after all?"

"I wish that were the case," he replied in a sober tone. "Answer me one question. Do you honestly believe your husband told you the truth when he said that he changed all four ball joints that night?"

She gripped the phone tighter. "I'd stake my life on it. Does this mean you believe someone tampered with the car?"

"I *know* someone did. I went out to the salvage yard and had the mechanic pull the ball joints from your Dodge Charger. All three were brand-new. We're lucky this much evidence still exists. Thanks to your discovery in the garage, there's every chance we're going to find the person who tampered with the car your husband worked on."

His answer sent shudder after shudder through her body.

"I've already ruled this out as a random act of vandalism committed while the car was parked outside in the rain. It takes knowledge and time by someone with an agenda who knows how to replace a ball joint in the middle of the night."

"So you're saying—"

"I'm saying your husband had an enemy who knew what he or she was doing," he broke in on her. "The tragedy is that it was raining when he took your car for a test-drive by that ditch. Otherwise your husband might have survived."

"I know," she whispered. "I've thought about that, too." Jessica shook her head. "I can't imagine who would have wanted to hurt Trent."

"Given time, that's what we're going to find out. This investigation is still in the early stages. I'll know more as the weeks go by and I'll phone you. Until then I want you to be very careful."

"I will," she said. "I said it myself earlier. If someone knew it was my car, it's possible they wanted *me* injured."

"I'm not at all sure about that, and see no reason for you to jump to that conclusion. I'm only asking you to be careful in terms of talking to anyone about this, Mrs. Fleming."

"Of course. Thank you for trying to help me feel better."

"What I'd like you to do right now is start thinking about your husband's life and the people who came in and out of it. Make a list of the ones you talked about during the recording along with anyone else you can think of. I have a gut feeling this criminal knew a lot about your husband and planned this out with exacting detail."

"It sounds that way." Her voice shook.

"I realize you don't think he had enemies, so look at it in terms of another person who could have been envious or in competition with him. Perhaps someone from his past with a grudge. Did you two have friends in common in high school?"

"You think this person might have known Trent as far back as then?"

"We have to consider every possibility. Were there ever times when he didn't get along with someone, be they male or female? A would-be girlfriend who was jealous of his interest in you? The receptionist at the dealership who might have been attracted to your husband despite the fact that he was married?"

Jessica walked around the kitchen. "Carol was their only female employee and she was married, but I realize that doesn't have to mean anything."

"It might not seem like a big thing to you, but to the other person it might have been the straw that broke the camel's back. Don't forget women are as capable of murder as a man. We can't rule anything out. I need more information than what is on the tape I made of our conversation."

She couldn't stop shivering. "I understand what you're saying."

"If possible, can you add ages, addresses and phone

numbers to the names and bring the list to my office on Friday at the end of the day? Your son is welcome to come with you. Tell him that after cleaning out your garage, you might have some things to donate to the sheriff's auction in July."

His resourcefulness amazed her. "That's a good idea. He won't think anything of it."

"I'll only need to talk to you for a few minutes."

"I'll start working on those names right away. Thank you for getting back to me so fast."

"Like you, I want to see this case wrapped up as soon as possible. Good night."

"Good night."

She hung up in a daze because she realized she hadn't wanted the conversation to end. Upset to be this distracted by him, she poured herself a fresh cup of coffee. This assignment was going to keep her up for a while. The first thing to do was call her mom and tell her what she'd learned. But she got her voice mail because her mother had gone out to dinner and a movie with a group of friends.

"Call me back. I have important news."

After getting paper and a pen from the study, she went back to the kitchen and began the arduous process of compiling a possible list of enemies. At ten after eleven her phone rang.

She clicked On. "Hi, Mom. Did you have a good time?"

"I did! But I want to know your news."

"Sheriff Granger called me. The bottom line is, he knows for a fact someone tampered with the car." The tone in his voice had left no doubt. "He's doing everything he can to find the person responsible and arrest them."

"Oh, honey."

"Awful, isn't it? I'm making a list of people who might have had it in for Trent. The sheriff wants me to bring it to his office on Friday. I was hoping you could help me think of people over the next few days. Honestly, I can't think of one person who would want to hurt him."

"Neither can I."

"Oh, and getting off topic, but just so you know, Wilma Morris will be watching Chase again at her house this summer. He and her son Joey get along great, and there's a new boy their age named Sam joining her group."

"That's wonderful!"

"I agree. Chase needs more friends when he's not at school, and he likes Wilma a lot. As soon as I drop him off at her house in the morning, I'll drive over to the shop and deal with any walk-ins. I don't have any appointments until Friday."

"I'm glad you've worked that out with Wilma. Why don't we hang up now so you can get some sleep? I'll think about this list of people and we'll talk in the morning."

"Sounds good. Love you."

She hung up the phone and went to bed. Maybe tomorrow more names would come to mind. To her chagrin, she didn't fall asleep for a long time. After finding the box of worn ball joints, she'd been living with the possibility that a crime had been committed. But to hear it confirmed by the sheriff was terrifying.

Who did she know who was so messed up in the

head that he or she would be willing to try to injure or get rid of Trent? And why?

Thank heaven the sheriff was conducting the investigation. Before she drifted off, the last thought on her mind was that she'd be seeing him Friday.

After hearing him talk about his niece and nephew, she had an idea he'd be a good father. One day he'd fall in love again and have a family.

Jessica realized she was lucky to have had Chase before early menopause struck. But it seemed so unfair when she had friends who were working on their second and third child.

Before long, Jessica was crying. After wallowing in self-pity for a while, she got angry with herself. What she needed to do was think about finding the evil person who'd tampered with the car that had killed her husband. Thank goodness Sheriff Granger was on the job. If he couldn't solve the crime, she figured no one could.

On his lunch break Friday, Holden stayed in his office to eat while he studied the police report on the Fleming case. Former Deputy Canaga, the investigating officer, hadn't mentioned looking at surveillance tapes from the dealership. By why would he? The accident happened out by the highway and he hadn't said a word about foul play being the cause. There was only mention of the defective ball joint.

Was it possible Mid-Valley had a surveillance camera overlooking the outside lot where clients' cars were left overnight?

He phoned O. J. Powell, Whitebark's fire chief, and was put right through.

"Holden—Welcome back! I understand you repaired a lot of fencing on your trip to Cody."

A chuckle escaped Holden's lips. Nothing was sacred with the guys. "My dad and I had some long talks, that's for sure."

"Promise me he didn't convince you to move back home."

"No. I like it here." Already this case for Mrs. Fleming had taken over his thoughts.

"That's the best news I've heard all day because we need you around here. What can I do for you?"

"I need a favor. Could you send one of your men over to the Mid-Valley auto dealership with the excuse that he's doing a routine check for fire extinguishers? You know the drill.

"While he's at it, ask him how many surveillance cameras he can see both inside and out, without letting anyone know. And when he looks around the parts department, ask him if he sees any Moog auto parts on the shelves. I need that information as part of my undercover investigation."

"Moog, huh?" O.J. laughed. "You old fox! I'll do it provided you let me in on what you're up to. As soon as he's done the job, I'll get back to you. How about lunch on Monday at the Blue Bird? One o'clock?"

"I'll be there. Thanks, O.J."

"Happy to oblige."

Holden left to pay a visit to the jail to talk to Lieutenant Fogarty. Because of what he learned there, he stopped at the bakery on the way back to the office to see Mrs. Allred.

"Sheriff—I'm so glad to see you! I've been worried

sick about Mike." She was the mother of the son in jail on a hunger strike.

"Don't worry. Yesterday I gave orders for him to be transferred to the hospital and a psychologist is working with him. Hopefully he'll cooperate. I've given instructions that you're welcome to visit him anytime."

"Bless you. Here!" She put half a dozen brownies in a carton and handed it to him. "I can't thank you enough."

"Let me know how it goes."

Holden downed two of the brownies on his way back to the office. For the next two hours, he worked his way through a packed schedule. Deep down, he kept waiting for five o'clock to roll around.

When it got to be six, he decided Jessica wasn't coming. Fighting disappointment, he left his office and started down the hall. But he didn't make it all the way because a cute boy and a stunning blonde woman came around the corner walking fast.

Their eyes met. "I'm sorry I'm so late. It was unavoidable. My last client was so upset with her hair color, I had to strip it and start over. I couldn't decide whether to call you to tell you I was running late, or just come as soon as I could. Forgive me."

"It doesn't matter. You're here now."

Her son stared up at him with warm brown eyes. "Are you the sheriff?" he asked.

He couldn't help but smile. "Yes. You must be Chase. How did you know?"

"Mom said you look like a sheriff should look."

Holden switched his attention to her. If he wasn't mistaken, she blushed.

"How come you're not wearing your cowboy hat?" Chase asked.

"That's a good question. When I'm out on the ranch, I wear it. But here at work I have another kind of hat I wear if I go on patrol. Come on back to my office and I'll show it to you."

Chase turned to his mother. "Can we?"

"Don't you remember we came to see him about a donation to the sheriff's auction?"

He nodded and they followed Holden, who told them to take a seat while he walked around behind his desk.

"Do you live on a ranch?"

Holden smiled. "That's right."

"We live on a ranch, too. Do you have a horse?"

"Yup. His name is Blackie."

"I don't like horses."

"How come?"

"They're so big!"

"Not all of them."

Chase lifted his head. "What do you mean?"

"Some are born little."

"But they get big! My dad loved horses, but he died."

Holden fought not to react. His throat had started to swell. "I'm very sorry to hear that, Chase."

"Me, too." He sighed. "Mom rides his horse."

"What's his name?"

"Bucky."

"Is that because he has buck teeth?"

Chase laughed. "No. Dad called him that because he's a buckskin."

His glance met Jessica's. "That makes perfect sense."

The boy looked around. "Where's your hat?"

"Right here." He pulled it out of his bottom drawer and put it on. Jessica looked as surprised as her son.

"That's a *baseball* cap!"

"Yup, except it says Sheriff. This is part of our new uniform. We don't wear cowboy boots, either."

"How come?"

"When we're out in the wind, our cowboy hats go flying off and our cowboy boots slip, so we wear hiking boots." He tugged on the visor. "We can't have our Stetsons blowing away, can we? This one stays put." The boy giggled. "Want to try it on?"

"Can I?"

"Sure. Come on over here."

He got up from the chair and walked over so Holden could put it on his head. This was Trent Fleming's son. The moment was surreal for Holden. It was too big for the boy, but if he wore it on the back of his head, it worked. "You look great in that, Chase. Show your mom."

Her son turned toward her.

Jessica's smile lit up Holden's insides. "I love it."

"I wish I had one like this."

"But only his can say Sheriff," she reminded him. "I know."

"Hey, Chase—have you had dinner already?"

"No."

"Neither have I, and I'm hungry. Do you like spaghetti?"

He whirled around with shining eyes. "Yeah!"

"Then keep the hat on and let's walk over to the Spaghetti Factory. They make these yummy meatballs. My niece Chrissy really loves them."

"How old is she?"

"Five."

"Hey—she's my age. Does she like horses?"

"Only her miniature horse."

He frowned. "What's 'miniature' mean?"

"A little horse."

"You mean a pony?"

"Nope. I mean one that's even smaller."

"Smaller—"

Holden realized Chase couldn't imagine it. He lifted his gaze to Jessica whose fabulous green eyes were lit up. "What do you say, Mrs. Fleming? Would you like to go to dinner? We can talk there as well as here."

"That sounds fun. I haven't eaten at the Spaghetti Factory for a long time." She handed him the list of names. He folded it and put it in his pocket.

Together they left the building and walked through the complex to the other side. He noticed that virtually every male in sight checked Jessica out. She looked fantastic in designer jeans and a soft pink blouse. The sun illuminated the gold highlights in her hair.

It felt good being with her and Chase. Normal. He hadn't experienced anything close to this kind of normal in over three years.

They entered the restaurant and were shown a table. They all decided to have spaghetti and meatballs. Chase ordered root beer while they drank coffee.

"School is out for you now, right?"

Chase nodded. "Yup. I go to playgroup when Mom works."

"That sounds fun. What do you do?"

"Stuff."

Holden grinned. "What kind of stuff?"

"We make puppets and do experiments. This week

we made different colors of slime. After lunch we have drawing time. And when we're good, our teacher lets us shoot lasers or watch *The Backyardigans* and *Arthur.*"

"Who's Arthur?"

"An aardvark, right, Mom?"

"Yes. He's a real character."

"I wouldn't mind coming to make slime with you," Holden said after his gaze met Jessica's. "It sounds a lot more exciting than what I do all day long."

Chase turned to his mother. "Do you think Wilma would let him come?"

She chuckled. "I don't know. You'd have to ask her."

Holden sat back in the chair, loving this conversation. "We still have a couple of hours of daylight left, so I have an idea. After we eat our chocolate sundaes, how would you like to go look at a miniature horse?"

One glance at their faces and he could see his suggestion had surprised both of them.

"Could we, Mom?" her son cried with excitement.

"Are you sure?" she asked Holden. "Do you have that kind of time?"

"Tonight is my night off. The people who run the miniature horse farm live right by my ranch. They have a son who takes care of Blackie when I can't get home. His name is Drake. Either he or his parents will show us around. I'll text him."

Chase was higher than a kite at this point.

Holden put his phone back in his pocket. "My brother and his wife bought my niece a horse from them and trailed it home for her as a birthday present."

"What a wonderful thing to do." This from Chase's mother.

"If you're ready, let's walk through the complex to my office. My truck is out in the back."

"Do we get to ride in your sheriff truck?"

"Yup."

Chase jumped up and down and the hat fell off. He reached over to put it back on his head. "Will you turn on the siren?"

"I'll do it when we get near my ranch."

Chapter 4

The sheriff was turning out to be her little boy's dream hero. In fact, this whole evening had come as such a pleasant surprise, Jessica was in a daze. All this time Chase had told her he didn't like horses, but she'd thought it was because he was scared of them. She'd hoped that in time he'd open up and talk about it.

Yet all the sheriff had to do was mention the miniature horse and her son showed no fear whatsoever. She would have never thought of a miniature horse to help him overcome his nervousness.

While Holden picked him up and helped him into the car seat installed in the rear, Jessica climbed into the front seat without his help. She wondered if he always drove around with the child's car seat, or only used it when his extended family came to visit. Whatever the explanation, he seemed to handle the situation as they took off for the south end of town.

Chase asked a dozen questions about how everything in the sheriff's truck worked. Jessica knew they'd gotten close to their destination when Holden made a left turn down a private road and she heard the siren blare. Her son was in heaven.

She laughed and looked at Holden, who smiled back. This time her heart did a definite leap. It surprised her that it didn't jump right out of her chest.

He drove them farther along the road until they came to the entrance of the other ranch. A sign posted Simpson's Miniature Horse Ranch. When the truck pulled around the rear of the ranch house, the siren started to die.

Jessica saw a young man in his late teens come outside on the back porch. He walked up to them with a smile.

"Hi, Sheriff. I heard you coming. Is it true someone wants to see our miniature horses?"

"That someone would be Chase Fleming."

Drake opened the back door. "Hi, Chase. I'm Drake. Come with me and I'll show you around."

With the hat still on her son's head, he glanced at her for permission. She opened her door. "I'll be right behind you, honey." Jessica got out and started walking. Holden joined her.

There were two corrals. One was large and contained two horses. Adjacent to it was a smaller one with three of the cutest little horses she'd ever seen. One was a sorrel and another was a palomino. The last one was a white Appaloosa with black spots and tail.

"They're adorable," Jessica cried.

Chase's eyes widened. "They're so tiny!"

"Yup." Drake grinned. "They're smaller than you.

Which one do you like best and you can lead him around?" He carried a small lead rope in his hand.

Her son looked up at Holden. "Which one do you like the most?"

"All of them. Shall we walk around and take a closer look? Then maybe you can decide."

"What about *you*, Mom?"

"I can't choose yet."

Jessica watched her son take hold of Holden's hand. Already trust was building with this exciting man. How sad his wife had died. It was even sadder he didn't have his own child to teach. He was a master.

The four of them went inside the corral and slowly walked around. Two of the horses ambled away from them, but the Appaloosa came toward Drake.

"That's right, Chocolate Chip. We're buddies, aren't we?" He put the rope around his neck.

"Chocolate Chip!"

Holden laughed at Chase's outburst. "He kind of looks like chocolate-chip ice cream."

"But he has black chips."

Drake grinned. "My father named him that when he was born. Dad has a sweet tooth. He named the palomino Caramel, and the sorrel Cinnamon Candy."

"That's funny."

"I think so, too, Chase. Do you want to lead him around for a minute? He's a very nice horse, gentle and friendly."

Jessica saw the struggle in her son's eyes before he took the end of the rope Drake had handed him. Just being willing to hold it was a huge step for her boy.

"Talk to him for a minute as you walk, Chase," Holden encouraged him. "Pretend you're taking your dog for a walk. Call him by his name. He'll go wherever you go because you're bigger than he is." How clever of Holden to keep reducing her son's anxiety.

Chase took ten seconds before he started leading him with the rope. "Come on, Chocolate Chip." Like magic, the horse began to follow. Pretty soon, the nervous lines around his mouth disappeared. "Look, Mom—"

She exchanged a warm glance with Holden before she said, "I'm looking, honey, and I can tell the horse likes you a lot. Just keep on walking around."

The other two horses started trailing them. By now, Chase had broken out in a huge smile. "Hey, look, Holden—they're following me!"

Holden chuckled. "They're happy you came to play with them." In an aside to Jessica he said, "The Pied Piper has arrived, Mom."

"That's exactly what I was thinking." Jessica pulled her cell phone from her purse and took some pictures.

They circled the corral twice before Drake walked over to him. "Do you want to ride on Chocolate Chip for a minute? The sheriff will stay right next to you."

Jessica realized that he must have texted certain information to Drake because the teen was fully aware of Chase's fear.

"Do you want to try? You don't have to."

Chase looked up into Holden's eyes. "Will you lift me?"

"Sure." In an instant, her son was sitting astride the tiny horse. Holden put the end of the short rope in his hand. "Tell the horse you want to go for a ride. Say, 'Giddyup!'"

The moment was surreal. Jessica held her breath

before Chase yelled, "Come on, Chocolate Chip. Giddyup!" She watched Drake give the horse's little rump a push and off they went while Holden walked at his side. The other horses followed.

Jessica's eyes misted over. This was the kind of experience missing in her son's life since losing Trent. She would always be grateful to the sheriff for helping Chase start to build confidence around horses. It was something she couldn't do in the same way. But after they'd been there a while, she felt they'd imposed on Drake too long. They'd all been having so much fun she didn't realize it was getting dark.

"Chase, honey? Guess what? We have to go home now. It's past your bedtime."

"But I don't want to go."

"I know."

"Tell you what, Chase," Holden intervened. "Drake will let us come over another time."

"Tomorrow?"

Jessica walked over to him. "No, Chase." She helped him off the horse. "Everyone will be busy. Have you forgotten I work part-time on Saturday?"

"I'll be here no matter when you want to come," Drake offered.

Holden darted her a glance. "Maybe I can arrange things at work tomorrow to free up my schedule to match yours for a few hours."

"Could you?"

The sheriff wasn't immune to Chase's plea because he said, "I'll see what I can do and call your mother in the morning."

Chase was so excited he jumped up and down before smiling at Drake. "Thanks for letting me ride on Chocolate Chip."

Even her son's manners were improving.

"Anytime."

They left Drake in the corral and walked over to the truck. Jessica climbed in on her own. Holden opened the door for Chase, who got up on his own and strapped himself in. After their host slid behind the wheel and they took off, she turned toward Chase. "Don't ask him to turn on the siren. It's too late."

"Okay."

Once again her eyes met Holden's. She figured he was relieved.

"I had the best time of my whole life!"

"So did I, honey."

"That makes three of us," Holden chimed in.

"Mom? Could we buy Chocolate Chip?" *Good heavens.* "Then I could ride with you."

Before Jessica could say anything, Holden spoke up. "There's just one problem with that, Chase. You're too big already to ride a miniature horse for more than a few minutes at a time. But he'd make a great pet. You could teach him tricks."

"That would be awesome!"

Before long, they'd arrived at the public parking area by the sheriff's office. After he shut off the engine, he turned to Chase. "If you want to ride with your mom, you should take a look at a couple of the Simpson's ponies. If we do go over there tomorrow, Drake will show you a couple."

"But they're bigger."

"That's right, but don't forget you're getting bigger every day, too."

"Oh, yeah." He'd made her boy think.

Not wanting to waste any more of the sheriff's time, Jessica got out of the truck while he took care of Chase. She headed for their truck and waited until he'd gotten into his car seat.

"Take care of your mom," she heard Holden say before he waved to both of them and entered the building.

Jessica was touched that he'd had the presence of mind to even think it, let alone say it.

"Mom? He left without his hat!"

"That's okay. We'll give it back to him the next time we see him."

Chase didn't stop talking as they drove home. This evening had been an adventure for her son, something exciting and out of the ordinary. He hadn't had a time like this since before Trent's death. Neither had she.

When they got home, he put on his pajamas and brushed his teeth. "Come on. Time for bed." She removed the hat. "You can't sleep in this. I'll put it on the bed post."

"I'll give it to him tomorrow."

Jessica took a quick breath. "Don't count on it. He's a very busy man. We'll have to wait and see." She reached for some of his storybooks and read to him until he finally fell asleep.

She watched TV for a few minutes before going to bed herself. Before she fell asleep, she wondered if Sheriff Granger would give her a call in the morning. Though she'd told Chase not to count on it, a part of her hoped she'd hear from him again.

The next morning while she was fixing breakfast, her phone rang. "Mom—maybe that's the sheriff!"

Of course her son had been listening for the call.

He'd come in the kitchen wearing the cap. She walked over to the counter and saw the caller ID. Her heart pounded before she picked up.

"Good morning, Sheriff." Chase was all smiles.

"I'd love it if you'd call me Holden. Would you mind?"

Her breath caught. "I'd be happy to."

"Does that mean I can call you Jessica?"

She chuckled. "I'd prefer it. Mrs. Fleming sounds so formal."

"Agreed."

"I want to thank you again for the wonderful outing last evening."

"I'd like us to do it again. Are you free next Wednesday after work?"

She knew what that meant. Today was out. She couldn't believe how disappointed she was. "I can certainly arrange to be."

"Several emergencies have cropped up that will keep me busy through the weekend and then some. But I've cleared my calendar for Wednesday if that would work for you. Can you be ready by five thirty?"

Her son's eyes were studying her. "That would be fine. I'll have picked up Chase by then."

"Here's my plan. I thought I'd come by your ranch with my trailer and we can load your horse. Then we'll stop at the horse farm, where Drake will make the miniature horses and pony available for Chase. If he wants to try riding the pony, then the three of us can take a ride on some trails leading from my ranch.

"But if he isn't ready for that, maybe I can talk Chase into riding on my horse with me. What do you think?"

To go riding with Holden? She gripped her phone

tighter. "I think you know what I think. We'll look forward to it."

"Not as much as I will." Those words sent a little thrill through her.

"Thanks for calling."

"Tell your son I'm sorry about today."

"He'll understand when I explain. Goodbye for now." She hung up.

Chase's face had fallen. "I knew he'd have to work."

"He can't help it, but guess what? He's going to come and pick us up on Wednesday after you're home from playgroup."

"But what if he can't?"

"He said he'd arranged for time off. Now, what do you say we eat? After I take care of Bucky, we'll go into town and do some shopping until I have to go to work. Holden mentioned that you're growing, and I can tell you are, especially your feet." He giggled. "You need new cowboy boots and jeans. Let's get going."

Already Jessica was thinking about Wednesday. While they were in town she figured she'd buy herself some new clothes, too.

Wednesday afternoon couldn't come soon enough for Holden. The second he walked out of headquarters, leaving Walt in charge, he drove home and changed into jeans. Once he'd eaten, he grabbed his cowboy hat and went out to the barn to saddle Blackie so he'd be ready.

After phoning Jessica to tell her he'd be there in twenty minutes, he hitched the trailer to his truck and took off. When he pulled around the back of Jessica's

house to the barn, Jessica and Chase were there waiting for him.

The adorable boy was wearing Holden's cap. Holden
jumped down from the cab. "Hey, Chase. Look at you
in your fancy new cowboy boots!"

"I got new jeans, too!"

"We look alike."

Chase ran up to him and took the cap off. "I forgot
to give this to you."

"It's a present from me. You keep it."

"But Mom says it's part of your uniform."

Holden darted her a glance. She'd put a lead rope
around Bucky, the gelding. "That's okay, Chase. I can
get me another one. It looks good on you and I like the
idea of you being a junior sheriff."

"Mom! He's made me a junior sheriff and says I
can keep the hat!"

"So I heard. Congratulations! Aren't you the luckiest boy in Whitebark?"

There couldn't be a more lovable boy around than
Chase. He looked a lot like his mother. Holden had
longed for a son or daughter, but Cynthia had been
taken from him too fast. He turned to Jessica who was
leading the horse to the back of the trailer. She looked
sensational in a Western shirt and jeans, wearing her
cowboy hat.

With a smile, Holden opened the door of his four-
horse trailer so she could lead Bucky to a stall and secure him. When that was accomplished, they all got in
his truck and headed for his ranch. Chase entertained
them on the drive with stories from playgroup.

This time when they arrived at the horse farm and
parked, he noticed Drake with a black pony on a lead

rope that had been put in the corral with the miniature horses.

Chase jumped out of the back and hurried over to the corral fencing, but he didn't go in. Jessica was close behind.

"Hey, Drake!" Holden called to him.

"Hi, everybody! Hey, Chase. Come on in. Chocolate Chip is waiting for you. So is Sparky."

Jessica took her son's hand, and they entered the corral. "That's another adorable name, Drake."

"Sparky fits him."

"He's not much bigger than the little horses."

"Nope. He's the perfect size for you, Chase."

Holden could tell the boy was giving Sparky a wide berth. But it delighted him when he walked right up to Chocolate Chip, who rubbed his head against Chase's chest, making him laugh.

"That horse likes you a lot," Holden commented. "If you'll sit down, he'll start to play with you." Pretty soon, laughter filled the corral. Chase lost any fear as he got up and ran around with the tiny horse following him for the next ten minutes.

"Do you want to pet the pony now? Drake has a hold of him."

After debating it for a minute, Chase walked over to the pony and imitated Holden who'd been smoothing the horse's neck and back.

"How would you like to ride him around?" Drake asked.

Holden knew that Chase was slowly losing his fear, but this was probably as close as he wanted to get to Sparky for today.

"I don't think I want to."

"That's okay. Maybe the next time you visit."

Jessica walked over. "That sounds great. Thank you, Drake. Now, I think we'd better go."

The three of them left the corral and got back in the truck. Holden drove them to his ranch and pulled around to the barn. He turned off the engine and looked over his shoulder at Chase.

"Your mother and I want to go for a ride. Will you ride with me on Blackie? I promise you'll be safe."

"Where will I sit?"

"Right in front of me."

It took at least a half a minute before he said, "Okay."

Victory! A small one, but a victory nevertheless. They were making progress.

After Holden's gaze connected with Jessica's, he got out of the truck and opened the trailer for her while he went in the barn for Blackie. Chase stayed by her as he brought his horse out.

"He's huge!"

"He needs to be in order to hold both of us." Holden mounted him. "Come on up."

Before Chase could make up his mind, Holden caught him and helped him settle in. "See how easy that was? You just lean back against me and we'll start walking. You can't fall because I've got you."

Jessica had mounted Bucky and sidled up to them. No rodeo queen could look as gorgeous, or appear more at home on a horse, than she did. "This is so exciting, honey," she said to Chase. "I've been wanting to ride with you for the longest time."

Holden lowered his head. "How are you feeling, Chase? Do you want to go for a ride, or would you rather get down? I don't want you to do anything that you don't like."

"Can we just walk around the corral first?"

"Of course."

Together with his mother, they circled around twice, taking it slowly until Holden could feel the boy's body relax. "You're doing great. I'm proud of you. Have you had enough, or would you like to explore outside the corral?"

"How far?"

"Just to that copse of cottonwood trees you can see in the distance. Then we'll come back."

"Okay."

Jessica smiled at her son, and they left the corral for the pastureland. Little by little, Chase started chatting. When they reached the trees and started back he said, "Can we go get a hamburger, Holden? I want fries in fry sauce, too."

"That sounds good. I could eat about five burgers, so I think we can manage it on the drive back to your ranch."

Chase looked over at her. "What do you want, Mom?"

"A cheeseburger and fries. It'll be our treat after everything Holden has done for us."

Before long, their pleasant ride ended. Jessica loaded her horse in the trailer while Holden put Blackie to bed with Chase watching him. When they drove away and came to a drive-through, she volunteered to go in for their food.

In addition to food for herself and Chase, Jessica ended up buying Holden three supersized cheeseburgers with all the fixings and root beers for everyone. It was dark by the time they reached her ranch and she unloaded Bucky. Holden walked with her and Chase to the barn where she put out fresh hay and water. Then he accompanied them to the back door where she turned on the lights both in the kitchen and outside.

Chase smiled up at him. "That was fun. Thanks, Holden."

"We'll have to do it again."

"Next time I might try to get on the pony."

Hooray! "If you don't, it doesn't matter. I had a great time, too."

"Chase? It's past your bedtime," Jessica reminded him. "Why don't you start your bath while I talk to Holden for a minute?"

"Okay." He ran off.

"You've got a terrific boy there, Jessica."

She removed her cowboy hat and smiled up at him. "You bring out the best in him. I'll never be able to thank you enough for what you've done for Chase. He's slowly losing his anxiety around horses."

A faint smile lit his lips. "In order to help him, I'd like to spend more time with the two of you when I can arrange it. To be honest, I always dreamed of having a child like Chase. He has to be a great comfort to you."

"He's my everything."

Holden tipped his hat. "I'll call you when I have more information on the case and we'll go riding again."

"We'll look forward to it. Good night."

"Good night."

Chapter 5

Thursday of the following week turned out to be a busy day at Style Clips. Millie had called in sick, so Jessica and Dottie had to do double duty to accommodate their clients. Jessica's client had just walked out the door when her cell phone rang.

She turned to Mrs. Avis, once of Millie's clients. "I'll be right back. Why don't you get in the chair?" Then she walked to the chemicals room in the rear and pulled the phone out of her pocket.

Holden's caller ID.

Jessica had almost given up that she'd hear from him this week. Every day since their last outing on Wednesday, Chase had asked her why he hadn't called. She kept telling him that a sheriff's job kept him so busy, it was a miracle if he had any free time. At least that was what she kept telling herself as one day, then another slipped away without hearing from him.

"Hello, Holden?"

"Hi. Remember me?"

She chuckled while she felt that deep voice reverberate through her body to her toes. The truth was, he'd been on her mind constantly, but she didn't dare tell him.

"It appears that crime in Sublette County is keeping our sheriff busy. It must be really hard to have any kind of social life." She wondered if he was involved with a woman. Jessica couldn't imagine him not being so.

"I signed up for it years ago."

"In other words, you wouldn't want to do anything else."

"Not so far. But I'm afraid I've interrupted your work. Could you call me back when you find some free time today?"

She blinked. "Sure. I have two more clients, then I'm through."

"What's your weekly schedule like?"

"This summer I'm working Monday through Thursday from nine to two, then I pick up Chase from playgroup. I also work part-time two Saturdays a month and keep Chase with me. My mother and the other two employees cover everything else."

"Do you take a lunch hour?"

"No. I usually just run upstairs to my mother's apartment and grab a bite between appointments. But you can call me anytime."

"I'll keep that in mind."

"I'll phone you as soon as my next client leaves, Holden." She knew this had to do with Trent's case.

"Terrific."

She hung up and hurried back to Mrs. Avis, more excited than she'd been all week. An hour and a half later, she went upstairs to her mom's apartment to phone him.

"Thanks for calling me back, Jessica. I wonder if you'd be willing to do me a favor."

"Of course. What is it?"

"I see on the list of people you gave me that Wes Bowen is the owner of the dealership. You didn't put an age down for him. How old would you say he is?"

"Probably in his seventies. I forgot to put that down."

"No problem. Have you met him before?"

"Every year we'd go to the Christmas party he threw for his staff at the Whitebark Hotel. I've probably talked to him half a dozen times. He and his wife came to the funeral and sent flowers. I always thought he was a very decent man."

"No doubt. Does he keep an office there?"

"I don't think so, but as you see on the list, his son Chuck is the general manager."

"How comfortable would you be phoning Wes and asking if you could talk to him in private? I need to keep this under the radar from his son and will tell you what to say."

"You mean now?"

"As soon as you can."

"I can do it after we get off the phone."

"I'd appreciate that. Tell him I have a judge's warrant to come in the dealership after-hours tonight to do some investigating of the accounts, personnel files and surveillance tapes. You'll have to tell him the truth— that someone tampered with your car and because of it, Trent was killed. That means his son is a suspect, too, and I don't want his son to know there's an investigation.

"This has to be kept confidential since anyone who was working at the dealership two years ago is a person of interest. Ask him to meet me there at 9:30 p.m. I'll show up out of uniform driving my dark blue Subaru. Hopefully no one else will be around. If that isn't convenient, then ask him to come to my office ASAP."

Obviously Holden was deep into the investigation. Jessica was glad she could help. "I'll call him right now and get back to you."

"Thanks."

"Okay, talk to you soon."

She left the shop and drove home to look up Wes Bowen's home phone number. After she'd eventually talked to him, she got back to Holden, who picked up on the second ring.

"I'm sorry this took so long, Holden. I had to wait for Mr. Bowen to call me back. He was clearly horrified when I told him the reason for the call. He said he'd meet you at nine thirty, but I could tell he's shaken up because he knows his son is a suspect."

"I'm going to reward you for this favor. Just so I'm straight about this—you're free on Fridays, right?"

"Yes."

"With tomorrow being Friday, let's agree to meet at the park next to the library with Chase. I'll take my lunch hour at one o'clock. We'll talk and make plans for another outing with him."

She pressed a hand to her heart. There was going to be another one. "We'll be waiting. I'll pack some sandwiches and drinks."

"Don't worry about food for me."

"Please, I want to. I'm so grateful for all your hard work on this case."

"Thank you. I'm making progress. See you soon. Say hi to Chase for me."

Jessica hung up and changed into a fresh outfit. After she picked up Chase, they were going to drive to the dealership. She was hoping one of the guys would make an offer on the truck.

When she pulled up to Wilma's, Chase came running out wearing his sheriff's hat, no doubt wanting to impress his friends.

"Hi, honey. You'll have to take the hat off because we're driving to the dealership. If anyone there saw it, they'd ask where you got it. It's a secret gift from Holden."

"But, Mom—" he started to argue.

"I promise to give it back after we get home. Right now I'm putting it in my tote bag for safekeeping." Holden was doing everything in his power to keep the investigation a secret.

Before long they pulled in at the service entrance. The door opened and Seth came out wearing the light blue dealership uniform, his long hair tied back in a ponytail. He smiled when he saw her.

Her mother had been right. He was definitely interested in her. Jessica could feel it. She'd never thought of Seth as anything but one of the mechanics. That would never change. The more he came on to her, the more she disliked the attention.

He sauntered up to her side of the truck. "Well, look who's here! How are you, Chase?"

"Good," he said in a quiet tone. Jessica noticed her son wouldn't look at him.

Seth zeroed in on her. "Do you need an oil change? I can do it right now if you want."

She shook her head. "I came to see if any of you

have decided to buy the truck. If not, I'm going to run an ad in the paper."

"Drive on in and I'll ask Danny to spread the word."

"Who's Danny?"

He leaned closer. In a low voice he said, "Eddie's new apprentice who doesn't know squat about cars."

"Are you going to buy it?" Chase's question came as a surprise to her.

"Maybe." He moved out of the way so she could drive in. He showed her where to park the truck. "Come into the waiting room."

Chase undid his seat belt and climbed out of the back seat. Seth stayed by her door to help. His arm brushed hers; there was nothing accidental about it.

"What kind of drink do you want? I'm buying. How about a Sprite?"

"Chase and I will share one. Thank you."

Jessica put an arm around Chase's shoulder and guided him to the chairs where they sat down. Her son stayed close to her. Seth handed her the remote so they could choose what they wanted to watch on the TV.

He also brought them a cold drink and removed the tab before handing it to Chase, but Chase wouldn't take it. Jessica reached for it. "Thank you."

"You're welcome. I'll be back."

Since her mother's comment, plus the fact that he'd bought Chase that toy truck, Jessica had begun to feel uncomfortable around Seth and she wished she hadn't driven out to the dealership after all. Chase was clearly unhappy and clung to her.

Over the next hour, each of the mechanics popped in to say hello. In the end it was Bryan who made an actual offer after driving the truck around for a while.

It wasn't as high as she'd hoped for. She might get more money if she ran an ad in the paper. "I'll think it over and get back to you soon."

Eddie bought Trent's tools on the spot and handed her a check without her breaking down in tears.

She'd decided not to sell the tool cart. Jessica had saved $1500 over a two-year period to pay for it and given it to Trent for his birthday. In the end, she couldn't sell it and decided to keep it in case Chase became a mechanic one day and wanted a souvenir of his father's.

With her business accomplished, she and Chase got back in the truck. After Chase was settled in his car seat, Seth closed her door. "I hope you're going to be there when I make my next appointment for a haircut."

This had to stop. She'd never let him down before… The fact that he was making something of it troubled her. Chase didn't like Seth's attention, either. He'd never had to share her with anyone except his nana.

"I'm there during my normal working hours, unless there's an emergency and I'm called away. Why don't you call the shop first to make sure?"

"Okay, I'll do that."

Jessica started the engine. "One more thing. I didn't realize you bought Chase that truck. I only found out recently. That was too generous. You shouldn't have done it."

He studied her features. "I wanted to. What would you say if the next time I come in for my appointment, it's at the end of the day? Afterward the three of us can go out for dinner, Chase's choice."

Her body cringed. How to answer him when she wasn't the least bit attracted to him and would never be interested? To make things worse, everyone at the dealership was a suspect in Trent's case. For several reasons she needed to be careful how she turned him down.

"I really can't say right now. We'll have to see." It was the only excuse she could think of while he'd put her on the spot.

"Sure," he said, but he didn't sound happy with her answer.

She was eager to get away and breathed a sigh of relief when she drove out onto the main street. Her next destination was the dump so she could unload the rest of the boxes in the truck bed.

How was she going to deal with Seth the next time he came into the salon? All the employees were suspects in Holden's secret investigation, including Seth. Under the circumstances, the thought of having any dealings with him, let alone cutting his hair, made her feel sick to her stomach.

"Are you going to go out to dinner with him?"

"No, honey. Not ever."

"Good. Can I have my hat now?"

Holden's hat.

Chase's comment brought her back to the present in a hurry. Jessica was excited to see Holden tomorrow. Too excited. Her son would be thrilled, as well.

"Sure." She opened her bag and handed it back to him. "Guess what? Holden called. We're meeting him at the park tomorrow for lunch."

"Hooray!"

All roads led back to the charming sheriff who'd taken up residence in Chase's mind. As for Jessica's...

* * *

While Holden had been arranging for a couple of prisoner transfers with the marshal's office after talking to Jessica earlier, someone knocked on his door.

"Sheriff Granger?"

Holden looked up. "Come in and sit down, Mrs. Sills." Jessica's good friend Donna had arrived on time. She was an attractive brunette. "I appreciate your taking the time to come to my office this late in the day, but I couldn't meet you before now and this is important."

"I admit I'm nervous to know what this is all about."

"As I told you on the phone, I'm doing an investigation on a case and need your input because you were good friends with Jessica growing up. You knew her husband Trent, right?"

"Oh, yes. I used to watch him at the rodeo. We were all good friends and went on double dates with my boyfriend, Rich. It's so horrible he died in that crash." Her eyes watered.

"That's why I've called you in. Trent was killed because someone deliberately tampered with Jessica's car, the one he'd been working on."

Her head lifted. *"What?"*

"Someone either wanted to cause damage, or wanted him or Jessica hurt. It might have been a person from his past, male or female. I'm hoping you can add information that might be helpful. That's why I asked if you had any yearbooks from your high school years. You might see a picture that jogs your memory."

"I brought my senior yearbook. It was all I could find."

"That's fine. Why don't you go through it with me?

If anything rings a bell, tell me. Do you remember any girls Trent dated before he met Jessica?"

"If he had a girlfriend before Jessica, I don't remember." Donna put the yearbook on top of his desk and opened it. "All I know is that they met in our English class and started dating." She leafed through the black-and-white pictures. "This is when Trent and Jessica were named king and queen of the Christmas dance."

Holden studied it for a moment. The two of them looked so young. Jessica was a beauty even back then. Chase had inherited some of his father's traits. "Was it a competition?"

"No. A popularity contest. Everyone just voted for whoever they wanted."

"So anyone could be chosen?"

"Yes. They got the most votes."

That didn't help Holden except to understand that they were both well liked. Anyone less secure might have resented Trent and been envious of his girlfriend. Or, it could have been a girl who was jealous of Trent's interest in Jessica.

"Here's the section for all the clubs. Our school had a lot of them. Jess and I were in the riding club, and this is a picture of the guys in the rodeo club. Trent's there front and center after he won his bull-riding event in the spring. I went to a few of them with Jessica."

"Do you recognize any of the other guys in this photograph?"

"Only the seniors." After a moment, she started pointing. "That's Larry, Tucker, Jed, Seth and Gary."

Seth?

"Will you find their class pictures so I can see their last names?"

She showed him each photo. Seth Lunt, with his long hair down to his shoulders, stood out because his was a name on the list Jessica had made for him. When Holden had asked her if all the dealership employees were from Whitebark, she'd said most of them had moved here. He wondered why she hadn't mentioned that Seth had gone to her high school.

Holden closed the book and smiled at Donna. "You've been more helpful than you know. Thank you for coming in. Please don't tell anyone about this visit—for your protection as well as Jessica's."

"I understand."

He walked her to the door. When she'd disappeared down the hall, he left for Angelino's to meet with some of the guys for dinner. But in truth, he would rather have been driving over to Jessica's.

After spending last Wednesday with her, the rule he'd imposed on himself not to mix pleasure with his work had gone right out the window. Being with Jessica Fleming wasn't a crime, but it was interfering with the rhythm of his life.

Last night when he'd finally gone to bed, he kept pounding his pillow trying to get comfortable, but sleep had eluded him because she was on his mind. When it got to be 1:30 a.m., he recognized the investigation was only part of the reason for his insomnia. Something was happening to him...

Unfortunately, his feelings were still so new, he didn't want to talk about her with his friends. He'd left the dealership after meeting with Wes Bowen, anxious to complete the investigation and identify the person who'd deprived the Fleming family of their husband and father.

Later that night, he'd headed back to the ranch, more than pleased with some of the information he'd uncovered. He could hardly wait to discuss it with Jessica.

Donna's was his last appointment for the day. After organizing his desk for the next morning, he headed to the city park. He was out of breath by the time he pulled into the parking area near Jessica's truck. June had come in warm and there were a lot of kids and adults out enjoying the sunshine.

Even so, Jessica commanded all of his attention in jeans and a leaf-green pullover. She sat on a picnic bench watching her son go down the slide. She'd placed a shopping bag on the table.

He got down from the cab and walked toward her, but Chase saw him from the top of the ladder and started waving. "Hey, Holden—watch me!" He went down on his stomach at slick speed. Chase had been wearing Holden's hat, but it fell off into the sand.

With a chuckle, Holden walked over and picked it up. "That was some trick. I think you lost something." He put the cap back on the boy's head, touched that he was still wearing it.

"I was afraid you couldn't come."

He liked the sound of that. "Let's hope I don't have to go out on an emergency."

"I don't want you to leave. We made a big lunch."

Chase was growing on him like mad. "What kind of sandwiches?"

"Mom fixed roast beef. I made peanut butter and jelly."

"Since you helped, can I have one of each?"

Jessica's son smiled up at him with those chocolate-brown eyes. "I told her you'd like peanut butter."

"You're right."

He eyed him intently. "Where did you get your first name? I never heard of it before."

Holden chuckled. The boy was an original. "When I was young I didn't know anyone else who had it, either. My mom liked the sound of it for some reason."

"My mom liked the name Chase, too. I don't have any friends with a name like mine, either."

"That makes us kind of special."

"Yeah."

Jessica had stayed put as she watched the two of them talking. After a minute, Chase came running over to her with a smile.

"Holden's here!"

Whatever the two of them had been talking about, Jessica could tell her son was delighted. She couldn't take her eyes off the striking, uniformed male striding toward her.

"Hello," he said in a deep voice. Those silvery eyes played over her, giving her a fluttery sensation in her chest.

Relieved that an emergency hadn't arisen to prevent him from meeting her, she got up. "We're glad you made it."

Though he'd come to discuss the case, she hoped that maybe he was glad to see her, too. He'd been on her mind continually since last Wednesday.

"Can we eat now, Mom?"

His question broke her concentration. "Sounds like a good idea since the sheriff is here on his lunch hour and doesn't have a lot of time. Come and sit down, Holden."

Chase plopped down next to him while she emptied the bag and laid everything out, including the sodas and salt-and-vinegar potato chips. Within moments, everyone was indulging themselves with fruit salad and sandwiches.

After Holden had devoured two sandwiches and half the bag of chips, he said, "This is the best lunch I've eaten in years."

"I told you he'd like peanut butter, Mom."

She laughed gently. "I think the whole world loves it."

They were just finishing up when Holden's phone rang. "Excuse me."

He got up from the table and walked a ways off. She knew he had to answer it, while Chase looked like he was going to burst into tears.

A few minutes later Holden came back and sat down.

"You don't have to go?"

"Nope." Holden smiled at her son. "I'm ready for dessert."

"Yay!" While they finished off some cookies, Chase's friend Joey arrived and asked if he could play. "I can't. We're eating with the sheriff. I told you he gave me his hat."

"Joey?" Jessica said to the boy. "This is Sheriff Granger."

"Hi, Joey. I hear you and Chase are friends."

The boy nodded shyly. Holden smiled at both of them. "Go ahead while we watch. I want to see you do some more tricks on the slide."

"Okay. Sometimes we go down double-decker. Don't go away, Holden."

"I'm not going anywhere."

When they ran off, Jessica looked at the gorgeous

man seated across from her. "That timing was perfect. While they're busy, how did it go with Wes Bowen?"

"I learned a lot. Thanks again for arranging it for me. He went through the shipping orders and found the ones for April. Three cartons of Moog ball joints had been ordered and shipped to Mid-Valley. But here's the telling point. A box of four was sold on May 14 to your husband."

She gasped. "That was the day before he was killed."

"That's right. Mr. Bowen found the receipt with your husband's signature on it. Apparently, the man you listed named John Agars remembered selling your husband four new ball joints. This morning I drove to Cora where Mr. Agars now works and he verified the sale. There's your proof."

"Oh, Holden." She shook her head. "I knew I wasn't wrong."

"No, you weren't. He also answered another vital question for me."

"What was it?"

"I asked him *when* your husband told him he needed new ball joints. He scratched his head and said it was the morning Trent drove to work in your car. Apparently Agars was in the employee parking lot getting out of his truck when Trent pulled in and asked if he had any Moog ball joints in the inventory. He said they were the best and planned to replace all the ball joints on your car."

"That's even more proof."

Holden nodded. "He told Trent he'd see what ball joints he had on hand. I asked Agars if anyone else had been around to hear them talking. He couldn't remember, but when he went inside and discovered several Moog boxes on the shelves, he went out to the bay with a box of four.

"Trent thanked him because he said he wanted to replace the old ones after work and take the car for a test-drive. Later, on his lunch hour, Trent went in the shop to pay for them."

Holden drew in a deep breath. "I asked if anyone else heard him talking with your husband after he took the box out to him. He said probably all the guys did because that morning everyone had arrived for work and they were all drinking coffee, getting ready for the day.

"Agars remembered there was a discussion about ball joints. Someone told him Mevotech and Duralast were good brands and cheaper. But the others said to stick with Moog."

Jessica stared at him. "Then it probably was someone from the dealership who did that to Trent."

"It's beginning to sound like it, but I've ruled out Agars. He's not a mechanic. There's something else I can tell you. Bowen gave me some evidence I have yet to go through. The surveillance tapes from that night were still there in a box. They will show anyone going in or out of the dealership. If the culprit was someone working there, they should be on the tapes."

Her face looked haunted. "It's so horrible that anyone would do that."

"Mr. Bowen said much the same thing. I reminded him that anyone could have gotten into the lot outside and tampered with the car, but no one has been accused of anything yet."

"That poor man must be terrified. Uh-oh. Here comes Chase."

Holden waved to him. "I'll text you this evening. Give me a call when he's asleep. There's more I need to discuss with you."

Chase came running over to them, cutting off any more discussion about the case. "Hi, honey. Did you have fun?"

"Yeah, but Joey had to go home with his older brother."

"We have to go, too. Will you throw these cans in the recycling? Holden has to get back to work."

"I wish you didn't have to go."

He hunkered down. "Tell you what. I'll talk to your mom. One day soon I'll have a whole day off and we can go on a hike. How would you like to do that?"

"I'd *love* it!" In a spontaneous gesture, he threw his arms around Holden, who hugged him back. Jessica couldn't believe it. Since Trent had died, she'd never seen her son show his affection like that to another man.

"We'll drive out of town and hike to the Elkhart Park Trailhead. My friend Cole spends a lot of time up in that area while he tracks elk."

"I've never been there," Jessica commented.

He glanced at her and smiled. "You'll love it," he said, then continued talking to Chase. "From there we'll follow the Pole Creek Trail alongside Faler Creek. You'll see almost every creature who lives there. When the forest starts to thin out, we'll have fabulous views of the Wind River Range to the north. If you're not too tired, Chase, we'll pass by Miller Lake for lunch, then walk back. There are lots of wildflowers in the meadows."

"Um, that sounds wonderful," Jessica said. "I haven't

done any hiking in a long time. I'll take my camera. If I get the right shot, I'll have it printed and framed." It would always remind her of her day with Holden.

"What a great idea! I remember your impressive photo collection. I don't get up in the mountains nearly as often as I want to. We'll take it easy so it's enjoyable."

"Do you think we'll see a wolverine?" Chase asked.

Holden laughed. "Like Logan from the X-Men?"

"Yeah."

"I think wolverines live in Canada and Alaska. But I'm sure we'll see some fascinating animals. Have you ever watched a yellow-bellied marmot come out of his burrow?"

"Yellow belly?" Chase giggled.

"That's right. Maybe we'll come across one. They live where we're going and whistle so loudly you won't believe it. I saw a big fat one the last time I was up there."

"What do they look like?"

"They're kind of a cross between a squirrel and a gopher."

"That's funny. I wish we didn't have to wait so long to go."

Holden smiled at Jessica before getting to his feet. "I'll call you. Thanks for the delicious lunch. Next time *I'll* bring it." He patted Chase's shoulder and took off for his truck.

After Holden disappeared, Jessica and Chase headed home. "How long do you think we have to wait until Holden can go?"

Jessica didn't want to think about it. "I've told you how busy he is. We'll just have to wait."

"Aw, darn."

"Darn" was right. Everything Holden said or did set him apart from the other men she knew. Later that night after she'd put Chase to bed, she phoned Holden. "You asked me to call, but is it too late?"

"Not at all. I'm back at work and have been discussing a schedule with Walt. How does next Friday sound for the hike?"

It sounded fine, but Chase would have a hard time waiting. "If you're sure you can take the time off, we'd love to go."

"Good. It's a date. Now before I let you go, I wanted you to know I've spoken with your friend Donna Sills. Was there a reason you didn't mention that Seth Lunt attended your high school?"

After her latest experience at the dealership, just the mention of the man's name made her shudder. "He *did* go to Whitebark, but that was so long ago that I forgot about it when I was putting down the information for you. We were never friends. I didn't know him back then. I'm sorry I failed to include it on the sheet."

"Don't worry about it," Holden murmured. "When I interviewed Donna at the office, she showed me some yearbook pictures."

"You're kidding! Most of those pictures are awful." Maybe it was silly of her, but she wasn't that thrilled with the way she looked at that age.

Chapter 6

Holden chuckled. "I'm just glad you can't see *my* year-book. You looked lovely in the photo of you and Trent being voted king and queen of the Christmas dance."

"I was afraid you saw that."

"Donna also showed me a photograph of the riding club with you on your palomino."

"I had to put her down a while back."

"That's not an easy thing to do. I also saw the rodeo club photo and asked her to identify the guys she knew. Seth was there, along with your husband, of course."

"In the three years we dated, my husband never talked about Seth. It wasn't until Trent had been working at the dealership for at least five years that he told me Seth Lunt, a guy from our high school, had just been hired as the new service writer.

"That was the first time I heard that Seth had tried to compete as a bull rider at some local rodeos during our senior year, but he just couldn't stay on and received bad scores. My husband said he felt sorry for him."

"You never saw Seth compete?"

"If I did, it didn't register."

He stirred in his swivel chair. "After Donna left my office, I contacted the Whitebark Rodeo Association president. He told me Seth Lunt didn't have the skills to go on the pro rodeo circuit. He stopped competing in local rodeos after receiving a series of disappointing scores."

"Hmm. I remember that Trent told me how surprised he was that Seth of all people had come to work at the dealership. He thought he would have gone to college in order to join his father's law firm one day. We both decided that some people just aren't interested in getting a higher education. Apparently working with his hands appealed to Seth."

Holden sat forward. "Except that he's not a true mechanic. What you've told me goes along with the research I've done on him, including Bowen's comments. Seth's grades weren't good in high school. He had to go to summer school to graduate. I also learned that before Seth was hired at Mid-Valley as a service writer, he'd worked at three different dealerships washing cars and as a parts person."

"I had no idea."

"There's something else important. Seth was divorced six years ago."

"That *is* news. I didn't know he'd been married."

"It only lasted a year. His wife asked for the divorce because he was in and out of work and took drugs."

"You have to wonder why Mr. Bowen hired him."

"Apparently, Seth was let go at the other dealerships

for either being late too often, for doing sloppy work or for failing their drug testing. I'm guessing he stayed clean because he was taken on at Mid-Valley and so far hasn't failed the drug test. At the South Mall dealership, they actually take the employees' fingerprints, but I can't get a copy without a judge's subpoena. That's my next item of business."

"You consider him a major suspect, don't you?" Jessica asked.

"It's looking like a stronger and stronger possibility. Let's consider that on the surface he had motive, opportunity and means, the first things you look for when a crime has been committed.

"Both he and your husband went to the same high school. They competed in the rodeo, but Seth failed to turn professional because he wasn't good enough. That alone could have been hard on him, plus the fact that your husband was so popular, he got voted in as king of the Christmas dance."

"You're right about that. Everyone liked Trent."

"Consider that your husband was taken on at Mid-Valley right out of high school, and with more schooling became a master mechanic."

"That was because his uncle Paul taught him everything he knew before he applied to work there."

"Again, Seth didn't have that skill to fall back on. I find it strange that he tried to follow in your husband's footsteps, but he has never attained the status of mechanic or come close to it. When you consider that there are hundreds of different jobs he could have interviewed for, I believe it's more than coincidence that he has tried to copy your husband."

"Holden?" Her voice sounded shaky.

"What is it?"

"There's another thing I forgot to tell you when I made out that list. For the first year after Trent's death, three of the guys from the dealership used to come to the salon to get their hair cut. Seth was one of them."

"That's interesting…"

"I knew that they were simply trying to be nice. They usually brought Chase a little treat. But for the last year or so Seth has been the only one to keep coming. I've been hoping he would stop."

Holden got to his feet. "You're still cutting *his* hair?"

"Yes, and lately he's been acting differently."

"Explain what you mean."

"He's come to the salon three times in the last couple of months. I thought it was rather odd because he has long hair and keeps it that way. Each time he said he just wanted a quarter of an inch trimmed. The last time he stopped by, I wasn't there because I had gone to your office. My mom said she or one of the other women would take care of him."

His hand tightened on the phone. "How did that go down?"

"Not well. This time he'd brought Chase a big fourteen-wheeler toy truck. It was an over-the-top gift. I was sorry he'd done it. When Seth found out I wasn't there, he left without letting anyone else cut his hair. Chase thought he was mad. My mom said she thought he's been attracted to me for a long time and was upset because I wasn't there."

Holden's jaw hardened.

"When I drove over to the dealership the other day to give the guys one more chance to buy Trent's truck, one of the other mechanics, Bryan, made an offer. Seth was on duty and hovered over Chase and me the whole time. My son didn't like it at all.

"Before we left, Seth asked me to be at the salon the next time he went in for an appointment. He suggested that if he came in at the end of the day, then we could go out for dinner afterward with Chase. Knowing what I know now since finding those ball joints in the garage, I can't tell you how the idea of being with Seth or anyone from the dealership fills me with terror."

"What did you tell him?" Holden demanded quietly.

"I told him that I couldn't say right now."

"That was the perfect answer."

"But I knew he didn't like it."

"Jessica, this news sheds a whole new light on the situation. I felt there had to be stronger motivation than just his jealousy of Trent. Now after what you've told me, I'm inclined to think Seth has been obsessed with *you* since high school."

"But I never even knew him!"

"That doesn't matter. You may not have remembered him, but the fact that *you* were voted queen of the Christmas dance and that you and Trent were a couple had to have played with his head in a big way. The fact that he continues to come for a haircut from you and brings Chase a gift like that speaks volumes."

"Holden, what am I going to do?"

"We'll talk about it on Friday during our hike. One more thing before we hang up. I have proof from the staff schedule Mr. Bowen provided that Seth was on duty the day your husband took your car in to work. That means he knew Trent's intention to change the ball joints." It was another bit of crucial evidence Holden needed to build the case against him. "In time

I'll learn his whereabouts the night your husband drove it out to the private parking area."

"Does that mean you're going to bring him in for questioning?"

Though Seth was the number one suspect in Holden's mind, he still had to keep the options open. If not Seth, another employee could have crept around the bay that night without Trent or Jessica knowing.

"Not until I've gathered a little more evidence. Promise me you won't go near the dealership or anyone there. Don't get back to Bryan about the truck yet, and do what you can to avoid talking to Seth if he calls for another appointment."

"I promise."

"We'll see each other on Friday. Be safe, Jessica."

"You, too."

For the next week Holden kept thinking about her comment. No one had ever told him to be safe before. When the next Friday dawned, he picked up his two favorite people, excited to be spending a whole day with them.

They stopped along the trail up the mountain and he hunkered down next to Chase. Jessica was behind them with her camera. "I heard a whistle. Keep looking next to that big rock." He handed the boy his binoculars. "That's where I saw the marmot before."

They stayed poised along the trail where there was a break in the trees. The sun, shining down on the Winds, streamed into the pocket while the chirping of birds and insects filled the air.

Pretty soon they saw movement and the marmot

peeked its head out of its burrow. "See his yellow belly?" Holden whispered as it stretched taller.

"It looks kind of like an orange cat," Chase whispered back.

"You're right."

"Does it know we're here?"

"Yes. They whistle when they sense danger."

"But we're not going to hurt it."

Holden loved the sweetness in this boy. "The marmot doesn't know that."

Suddenly, a blue jay flew toward a copse of trees, startling the marmot. Out came such a loud whistle from the marmot that Chase fell back against Jessica. They all laughed and the marmot disappeared into the burrow.

Chase handed Holden the binoculars. "Do you think he'll come out again?"

"Sure." He put them around his neck. "After we eat lunch and come back down, we'll catch him taking another sunbath."

"Do they really take sunbaths, Mom?"

She stood up. "I think animals are like people and enjoy getting in the sun. Let's keep going. Maybe we'll see another one."

They eventually reached Miller Lake where Jessica took a lot of pictures. "Looks like other hikers have had the same idea," Holden said. "But I bet none have as good a lunch as ours. These peanut butter sandwiches you made with strawberry jelly are the best, Chase."

"Thanks."

Jessica flashed Holden a glance. "I happen to love your super-duper bologna, ham and cheese sandwiches." They all agreed salt-and-vinegar chips were their favorite kind. After they'd emptied the bag, Holden produced doughnuts for dessert.

Chase devoured his. "Do you think if we left part of a doughnut by the burrow, the marmot would eat it?"

A laugh broke from Holden. "Tell you what. Let's do it and see what happens."

After they drank from their water bottles, they trekked back to the spot that Chase couldn't wait to reach. Holden handed him half a doughnut that didn't have icing. "I don't know if it would like chocolate. Go ahead and put it next to the burrow. We'll see what happens."

Chase showed no fear placing the doughnut near the hole before the three of them hunkered down in the same spot as before and waited to see what would happen. After ten minutes Holden decided the marmot wasn't going to come out. "What do you think?" he whispered. "Shall we go on waiting?"

"Just a little longer." Chase had hold of the binoculars.

Holden couldn't resist his plea. He wished this day would go on forever.

Five minutes passed before Chase drew in his breath. "There he is—"

Once again the marmot poked its head up and looked around. Its movements were quick. "He took it!" Chase cried. But the sound of his voice carried and caused the marmot to disappear. "Heck—I wanted to see him eat it."

Jessica hugged him hard. "I don't think he wanted to share it with that blue jay perched in the trees."

More laughter escaped Holden. "I bet that yellow belly has never tasted anything so good."

"Can we come up here again and feed him something else?"

"Why not?"

"Wait till I tell Joey."

They started to walk down to the truck with Chase leading the way. After driving back to his ranch house to freshen up, they went to see the latest animated movie downtown. After that, Chase wanted to go to the Spaghetti Factory again for dinner.

Full of good food, they arrived back at Jessica's and went inside. Holden wanted time alone with her. He hoped Chase was tuckered out and wouldn't have a problem going to bed. But he was full of questions.

"Mom? Did you tell Holden we're going to sell the truck?"

"Yes. I told him Bryan made an offer."

"Are you going to let him buy it?"

"Yes. I talked it over with Nana yesterday. His offer was a little lower than I'd hoped to get, but I don't feel like going to all the trouble of running an ad and being on hand to show it to potential buyers."

"Now we can buy a new car, huh, Mom?"

"Yes, darling."

"I'd say you're a very lucky guy, Chase."

He stood next to Holden and looked up at him. "We went to my dad's work last week."

He fastened his attention on Jessica's son. "I bet it reminds you of him."

"Not anymore. I don't like going there." Holden's gaze fused with Jessica's before Chase said, "Hey— do you want to come to my nana's shop? Mom will cut your hair. She's really good at it."

"I bet she's the best." That boy was still in the dark

and Holden wanted to keep it that way. But the chasm was opening, revealing an unspeakable picture of potential evil where Seth might be concerned. He saw the agony on Jessica's face.

"Holden has his own person to cut his hair," she blurted. "Come on, honey. Let's get you in the tub."

"But we don't have to go anywhere tomorrow."

"That's true, but Holden has to be on call at six in the morning. It's getting late and he still has to drive home."

"I know." He stared up at him. "Thanks for the hike. I had the best time of my whole life!"

The boy had said the same thing after their last outing. "We'll do it again soon. Maybe next time we'll leave the marmot a cookie."

Chase giggled before giving him a hug and running out of the living room.

Jessica followed. "I'll be back the second he's in bed."

While she was gone, Holden phoned Walt for an update and a discussion of their work schedule before hanging up. Tomorrow when he got back to the office, he'd look at the dealership surveillance tapes.

He would also stop by forensics to talk to Cyril about the fingerprints left on the ball joints. Holden particularly wanted to know if any had been lifted off the Duralast ball joint. That was the one the criminal had put on the car.

At that point he would run the prints through the Integrated Automated Fingerprint Identification System to see what he could find. Following that, he'd go through the names of all the employees and find out if any had criminal records. Perhaps there'd been drug testing and fingerprints taken. You never knew what would turn up.

"Holden?" He'd been so deep in thought he hadn't realized Jessica had come back in the living room. "Sorry it took so long. I think Chase had too good of a time today."

He smiled. "I feel the same way, but now we have to get back to something serious before I leave."

"I know." She sank down on the couch opposite him.

"Tomorrow being Saturday, why don't you call Bryan in the morning and ask him to come over here after your work. Tell him to bring a cashier's check. When he shows up, try not to touch it. I want to examine it for fingerprints. As for the gift Seth gave Chase, did it come in a box?"

"Yes."

"By any chance do you still have it?"

"Maybe. It would be at my mom's."

"I'll come by your house sometime Monday after your work and pick up the check. If you find the box, I'll pick that up, too, and ask forensics to put a rush on them for fingerprints. One of the deputies will bring the check back to you on Tuesday morning so you can put it in your bank."

"Thank you."

"Now about next Friday. If you don't have other plans I was thinking we could take Chase to the Simpson's farm in the afternoon and see if he'll be willing to get on the pony and go for a ride with us."

"That would be wonderful! Afterward I'll fix dinner for us. It's my turn to treat."

Her words were music to his ears and a great deal more, but he didn't dare examine the emotions flowing through him yet. "I'll call you before then to make sure our plans are set. See you Monday to pick up the check, but I don't know the time yet."

"That's fine. I'll be here after I bring Chase home from playgroup."

At the door he turned to her. "If you want to know the truth, I had the time of my life today, too."

When Bryan came by on Saturday evening, Jessica was fixing corn dogs for dinner. She invited him in the living room to give him the truck title and the keys. He, in turn, pulled an envelope from his pocket and showed her the check before putting it back inside.

"Just leave it there on the table, and I'll walk you out to the truck."

"Thanks, Jessica. I've needed another vehicle. This truck is perfect."

"It's been a good one."

He was so nice, she couldn't imagine him doing anything criminal. But pleasant as he was, she had to remember what Holden had said. There was a strong possibility that he or Seth or any of the guys might have hated Trent enough to try to hurt him or cause him grief. Holden hadn't proved who'd tampered with the car yet, but she knew he was getting closer to discovering the truth.

Chase walked out to the driveway with her. They watched until Bryan had backed the truck out to the street and driven away. His wife waved to them from their car before following him.

"There goes Dad's truck," Chase said. Jessica hugged him hard. She'd heard the little tremor in his voice. "Are we going to get our new Toyota tomorrow?"

"Tomorrow is Sunday. We'll probably go on Tuesday. Nana will drive us to the Toyota dealership. What's nice is that our garage is ready." Jessica still couldn't believe that in cleaning it out, she'd inadvertently set off the search for the person who'd caused Trent's death.

Together they went back in the house for corn dogs and salad. Then Chase took his bath and got ready for bed. She read him stories but it was hard to pretend nothing was wrong, not when she was counting the hours until Holden came over on Monday night.

When she phoned her mom, she was disappointed to learn her mother had thrown out the box that held the truck Seth had bought. But it couldn't be helped.

While she was straightening up the house, Holden texted her, wanting to know about Bryan. It sent a dart of excitement through her. She texted him back, embarrassingly aware how eager she was to hear from him.

The cashier's check is here on the coffee table. I never touched it. He left in the truck. All is well. But Mom threw out the box.

He answered back. No problem about the box. So far, so good. See you Monday, and don't forget our plans on Friday!

She sent one more message. I hope you like fajitas.

His response was an emoji of a round face with a huge grin. It made her smile.

In a short time Jessica had become infatuated with the sheriff for reasons that went far beyond pure physical attraction. Being with him made her feel alive again.

When Monday evening came, Chase ran outside to greet Holden when he pulled up in the driveway. Before she knew it, Chase was riding on his shoulders when he came in the house. For a little while, her son's happy laugh helped her forget the real reason why Holden had come. With a gloved hand, he picked up Bryan's envelope so he wouldn't contaminate the evidence.

While they stood in the living room talking, his phone rang. After answering it he darted her a glance. "Got to go," he said, ruffling Chase's hair. "See you on Friday." In the blink of an eye he was gone.

"I wish he didn't have to go."

So do I. "His job is to help people in trouble."

"He took off like the Flash!"

"He certainly did," Jessica agreed, trying to hide her disappointment. "Come on. Let's get ready for bed. We're going to go get a new car in the morning."

"Hooray. I can't wait for Holden to see it."

Holden… Holden.

Later, when he had fallen asleep, she turned on the TV in time to hear the ten o'clock news. There'd been a shooting involving a Whitebark cattle ranching family. She shuddered when she learned that it had happened near Wilma's ranch.

According to the girlfriend of the suspect, her boyfriend had barricaded himself inside the ranch house with his parents and she'd heard shots. But there were no details yet.

Jessica couldn't remember the last time she'd heard of a shooting here in Whitebark. Her thoughts flew to Holden who would be in charge. She shuddered again and turned off the TV to get ready for bed. His could be a fatally dangerous occupation. She didn't want to think about that or the investigation into Trent's death tonight. She'd had the most wonderful time last Friday and wanted to savor it.

Holden flew down the highway to the Crosby ranch where a mass of police cars and several ambulances had already assembled. As he got out of his truck, Deputy Larson walked over and apprised him of what was going on.

"The suspect is barricaded inside and threatening to kill himself if we don't let his girlfriend go in. She's being detained while we talk to him. He's fired three warning shots."

"Keep him engaged. Cover me while I go around the back." Holden took off at a run to where another deputy was stationed at the back porch. With his help, Holden climbed to the second floor and broke a window to get inside. He stole through a bedroom and hall to slip down the stairs.

From the foyer, he could see two bodies on the floor of the living room. The suspect was stationed at the front window with a rifle. He'd broken the glass.

Holden crept up behind him and knocked his legs out from under him. His rifle went off as his body buckled to the floor. Holden quickly surprised him with a hammerlock and cuffed him.

Using his phone, he called for backup. Within seconds three deputies rushed in and the standoff was over. A domestic dispute turned violent had left both of the suspect's parents dead. Holden arrested the son and he was hauled off to jail in a patrol car. After spending another twenty minutes on location, he left for his ranch and grabbed a bite before going to bed.

On Tuesday, Jessica had become the owner of a brand-new Toyota. With her mother's help, they'd taken Chase's car seat to the dealership where it was installed in the back. After hugging her mom, who had to get back to work, Jessica took Chase for a drive. She loved it. So did he.

They stopped at the Dairy Ann drive-in and went inside for lunch. Then she drove him to his playgroup. "See you after work, honey."

On her way back to Style Clips it hit her hard that her old life was gone and a new one had begun. Though she'd sold Trent's truck to Bryan—who she still couldn't believe could be responsible for her husband's death— she didn't feel any expected pain associated with the loss of it.

A bright new day had dawned and she knew why as she parked the car behind the shop. Her heart pounded as she realized she and Chase would be spending Friday evening with Holden. Jessica feared she was falling for him. No, that wasn't exactly true. She *had* fallen for him.

What had her mother told her? Every available woman in Whitebark was crazy about him. She closed her eyes for minute. It seemed she'd joined that legion without realizing it.

She imagined that any of those available women would love to be married to a man like Holden and have children with him. Children *they* could give him. That was something Jessica couldn't do, unless as the doctor said, she was one of those rare cases where a miracle happened. How she envied those other women.

The smile she'd been wearing faded as she locked her new car and went inside the salon to get to work.

Chapter 7

Since the previous Friday night, Holden had been working feverishly with a delegation of deputies newly assigned to deal with wild animal control issues. Coyotes were preying on sheep and cattle around the Whitebark community and were becoming a major problem for the ranchers. Through Friday to this Thursday they'd been out on back-to-back patrols to rid the ranches of the predators.

Near the end of the day on Thursday, Holden returned to headquarters and issued outstanding warrants that needed to be served by the marshal. Following that, he took a four-hour turn patrolling an arterial road that led to the highway where too many speeders caused accidents.

As he watched for speeders and gave out tickets, his mind was on Jessica. Tomorrow morning he'd dedicate his time to her husband's case and by the afternoon he'd be with her. It amazed him how much he'd changed since meeting her.

Every night when he went to bed, he had trouble falling asleep as his mind raced with thoughts of Jessica. He wanted to be with her and Chase whenever possible. But he couldn't think about spending true quality time with the two of them—like taking them on a trip to Cody—until he'd solved Trent's murder.

On Friday morning, he went into the office and first worked through a pile of paperwork relating to the Crosby shootings. With that done he could at last get to work making copies of the Mid-Valley dealership personnel sheets with the employees' pictures. Holden would need them for identification because he planned to go through the box of surveillance tapes he'd taken from the dealership next.

After pulling the two tapes he needed, he gathered the papers and walked back to the department's lab to run the tapes through the scanner. With the picture ID, he could match names and faces.

The tapes at the dealership had run continually on a time clock. He put in the one that covered the service writer entrance and started watching the May 14 tape from the 6:00 a.m. time stamp.

At two minutes after 8:00 a.m., the bay door opened and three figures appeared in dealership uniforms. Two stood farther away so he couldn't identify their faces. The other one walked to the work counter. He had long hair. Only one of the employees had shoulder-length hair like that, proving Seth Lunt had been on duty.

Holden watched the entire tape. By 5:15 p.m., there was no more activity and the bay door was closed.

Without wasting a minute, Holden fed the other tape into the scanner covering the employees' back exit and watched while it covered the entire day of May 14. One mechanic he identified as Bryan left the place at two o'clock in the afternoon. No more people went out until five. Little by little everyone who left by the back exit had gone by 8:30 p.m.

The lighting wasn't as good that late, but so far he hadn't seen a sign of Seth. He might have gone out the front door. Holden kept watching. Someone else left at ten thirty. As far as he could tell it was the general manager's son. But he could see only his back and head in silhouette.

He kept running the tape. At 2:10 a.m. on May 15 another figure left out the back exit. All he could see was the back of a man with *long hair*.

Seth!

The culprit had hidden out somewhere in the building and waited until he knew no one would ever see him. If he carried tools, Holden couldn't tell. He was incredulous to think this evidence still existed! There was no more activity that day until 9:30 a.m. when one of the mechanics went out.

Holden quickly ran the other tape through for May 15, watching for the dealership to open again. At 8:00 a.m. he saw the bay door lift and two people appeared. One of the figures was Eddie, the other Seth. He'd returned to the scene of the crime as if he'd done nothing!

The fact that he'd been on the premises and had gone out the door during the night was crucial evidence. Since Gil would report for work on the following Monday morning, Holden marked the places on both tapes and left him a note to enlarge these parts.

He asked him to make paper copies and bring them to Holden's office the second he was finished. This was top priority.

By three in the afternoon, he'd gone home to shower and change. Earlier, he'd phoned Drake and asked him to have Sparky saddled in case Chase was willing to get up on him and ride around. They'd be there in about an hour.

Like déjà vu, Chase was waiting for him when he pulled around the rear of the Fleming ranch later that day with the trailer.

"Holden—" He came running to him.

In that moment, Holden knew he loved the boy and swept him up in his arms. Chase had worked his way into his heart. "Are you ready to go for a pony back ride?"

"Yup. I promised Mom I would."

Jessica emerged from the barn with Bucky. When their eyes met, it felt like all the wind had been knocked out of him.

"Hi." He tipped his hat.

"Hi, stranger," she answered with an enticing smile on her lips. She looked amazing in her cowboy hat and Western vest with fringe. He hadn't seen her since Monday night.

"It *has* been a long time." Much too long.

There was so much to tell her, but it would have to wait until they could be alone later.

She walked her horse into the trailer while he opened the door for Chase to climb in the truck. The first thing he said when they left for the Simpson's ranch took Holden by surprise.

"Joey's mom told us her neighbors got killed. Did their son really shoot them?"

The news of the shooting had impacted the whole town. He exchanged a concerned glance with Jessica. "I'm afraid so."

"Did you put him in jail?"

Holden's hands tightened on the steering wheel. "Several police officers took him away."

"Was he crazy?"

"No, just very, very unhappy."

"Oh. Is that why people kill people?"

The subject was touching on something too painful for Jessica. For Holden, too. "I think that's the reason most of the time, but let's not worry about him. How do you like your new car?"

"I love it! Wait till you see it. Mom? Can we take Holden for a ride in it?"

She flashed Holden a smile. "Only if he doesn't mind me driving."

"She's a good driver, Holden!" Chase said.

He laughed. "I believe it after the way I've seen her ride Bucky. He's a high-spirited horse. Not everyone could handle him the way she does."

"So you've noticed," she said under her breath.

"I notice a lot more than you think I do," he came back in an aside. His comment brought a flush to her cheeks.

"Hey—there's Drake and Sparky! Where's Chocolate Chip?"

"Probably in the barn eating with the other miniature horses."

They alighted from the truck and walked inside the larger corral, greeting Drake who steadied Sparky.

Holden could tell Chase was nervous, but he didn't shy away.

"Do you want to get on him?"

Chase nodded.

"Then up you go." Holden lowered him into the saddle and put the reins in his hands.

Jessica smiled up at her son. "How does it feel?"

"It's different than riding with Holden. Sparky isn't as tall."

"No, honey. He's your size."

"Holden? Will you walk around with us?"

"I'm right here. Hold the reins, but not too tightly."

"Giddyup, Sparky."

With a pat on the pony's rump, it started to walk. Holden stayed right next to him. The pony knew where to go and just started making wide circles around the corral.

"You're doing great!" Jessica called out.

"It's fun!"

Holden's throat swelled with pride that Chase was conquering his fear. After three times around he said, "Do you feel like going on a ride with your mother and me?"

"Okay. Can we take Sparky in your trailer?"

"How about it, Drake?"

"No problem."

"I'll stay in the stall with him," Jessica offered.

She walked Sparky inside the trailer to the stall next to Bucky. Holden helped her tie him. They stood close together. He could see a little nerve throbbing at the base of her throat. "See you shortly."

"This is so exciting, Holden." In the dim light of the

trailer, her green eyes dazzled him. "I never thought this day would come."

"Chase is a brave boy."

"With an incredible mentor."

The tension between them was so thick, he came close to lowering his mouth to hers. But remembering that Chase was waiting outside the trailer, he turned on his heel and got out of there fast.

In five minutes, they'd reached his ranch. Chase went into the barn and watched Holden saddle Blackie. When they came out again, Jessica was there astride Bucky, holding the lead on Sparky.

Once again, Holden lifted Chase onto the pony and put the reins in his hands. Then he mounted Blackie and the three of them started walking with Chase riding between them.

"Hey—Sparky knows where to go!"

Holden grinned at Jessica. "He feels safe and is following us."

This time they went twice as far as before and talked about Chase's father. "My dad used to be a bull rider. We have a lot of pictures."

"He was one of the best, honey," Jessica said.

Chase's head swerved to Holden. "Did you ride in the rodeo?"

"Yes, but I just had fun with my brother doing tie-down roping. We weren't professionals like your father. I saw a picture of him in a high school yearbook your mother's friend showed me. He was a real pro."

"Maybe one day I'll be in the rodeo, too."

"With the way you're handling Sparky, I wouldn't be at all surprised."

They headed back to the Simpson's ranch and returned the pony to Drake. Holden thanked him before they drove to the Fleming ranch for dinner.

Jessica had said she was making fajitas, but she'd prepared a bunch more delicious items including the best guacamole dip and sopapillas he'd ever tasted. After dinner they went for a short ride in the new car.

It was a novel experience letting her chauffer him around. "This is a great car you bought. Who chose the color? You or Chase?"

"We both agreed that we liked silver the best, didn't we, Chase? So the choice was easy."

"I like your taste."

Afterward they came back and played Go Fish. Finally, Jessica said it was time for Chase's bath and bed.

"Do I have to?"

Jessica gave him a kiss on the cheek. "You do."

He got up and hugged Holden.

"I'll be back," Jessica murmured.

While they were gone Holden returned some calls until she reappeared.

He hung up and eyed her intently. "Let's talk. I've got a theory and want you to hear me out."

"Can I get you something to eat or drink first?"

"After that terrific meal, I couldn't eat a thing, but thank you."

She sat down on the end of the couch while he drew up a chair near her. He leaned forward with his hands clasped between his knees and told her what he'd discovered on the surveillance tapes.

Jessica let out a cry. "You *saw* him sneak out of the dealership in the middle of the night."

He nodded. "I'll show you photographs if you want. If I'm right and Seth has had a thing for you since high school, then it makes sense that he's been stalking you, coming to your shop for a hair trim."

A moan escaped her lips. "This is so horrible."

He reached out to squeeze her hand, wanting to do much more, but this wasn't the time. "I can only imagine what you're going through. No one wants this to go away more than I do. The problem is, without proof he tampered with the car, this is still just a theory. We both know everyone is suspect, but for the time being, Seth is the leading person of interest."

Jessica nodded.

"In my mind it doesn't make sense that Seth has been in and out of jobs until you look at his choices of places to work. Each one has been at a dealership. I've thought all along that whoever did this was patient and calculating. Seth fits the profile of eventually being hired on at Mid-Valley. That brought him close to Trent and, indirectly, to you.

"I agree. I'm scared, Holden."

"I know you are, and I can't blame you for worrying about the next time he comes to the salon. I'm doing everything possible to close in on this investigation. Just be aware that Seth most likely wants a relationship with you. The more I learn about him, the more I'm worried about your safety."

She sat forward. "Much as I hate to admit it, I know you're on to something vital. In hindsight I can see that he's been interested in me since the funeral."

"When did he first come to the salon?"

"Maybe a month after the funeral he and the guys called to make appointments for haircuts. Eddie and Bryan eventually stopped coming in, but as I told you,

Seth has remained a loyal client and always asks about Chase."

Holden nodded. "It still doesn't make him guilty without solid proof."

She stood up. "I've been going over it in my mind. Since you told me he'd been married and that his first wife divorced him, it's clear he's had a lot of rejections that must have started back in high school or even before. Maybe he'd hoped to be voted king of the dance. Then there was the disappointment of being unable to compete in the pro rodeo. That's probably when he got started on drugs."

"Maybe," Holden muttered. "Or maybe he had a bad family life. It's all theory." He got to his feet. "I wish I could stay longer, but I was on the phone a few minutes ago and have to get to the jail pronto. I'll call you tomorrow and we'll talk more. Thanks again for a wonderful dinner."

"You're welcome."

"Please remember one thing. Assuming Seth is the one responsible for Trent's death, every day he's free puts you in greater jeopardy, so be on your guard."

"I promise," Jessica said as she held the door open and watched him leave.

Jessica was between customers on Monday afternoon when her cell phone rang. "Holden?" she said when she saw the caller ID. "Thank goodness it's you. I've been so anxious to talk to you."

He heard the panic in her voice. "What's happened?"

"Seth phoned the salon last night and left me a message. He wants to take Chase and me to dinner on Tuesday evening. This time he didn't even ask about a haircut. Because he doesn't have my cell phone number, he can't reach me any other way."

"Jessica, you and I need to meet this evening."

"Does that mean you've learned more?"

"I'll answer all your questions when we see each other. Do nothing about Seth until we've talked. Can you get a sitter for Chase? I want us to be alone to discuss the case."

"Yes. I'll ask my friend Donna if she can watch him. She has a daughter, Lily, who Chase likes to play with. If Donna can't help, my mother will do it, though I hate to impose on her."

"Understood. I'll come by the house at six and we can eat dinner at my house. I know Chase won't be with us, but I want to treat you with dinner."

Her eyes closed for a second. He wanted to take her to his house. "That sounds ideal." Her voice trembled. "I'll be ready." Jessica wanted to tell him she couldn't wait, but she held back.

"Perfect," he murmured. "See you tonight."

After he hung up, she phoned Donna who was happy to have Chase come over. They chatted until Jessica's next client came in, but she wasn't free to tell her friend about the case.

Later in the day, she picked up Chase. He was excited when she told him he was going to have a playdate with Lily that night. While he ate, she showered and put on a green-and-white-print sundress with a jacket.

"Where are you going?" he asked when they pulled up in front of Donna's house.

She told Chase the truth—that she planned to meet with Holden.

A smile broke out on his cute face beneath the sheriff's cap. "Tell him I can't wait to see him again."

"I think he knows that already." She was living for it, too. "See you later. Have fun with Lily."

He got out of the car seat in the back and ran up to the front door. Donna and Lily opened it and waved before Jessica drove off.

Holden's Subaru was parked in front of her house when she pulled into her garage. Just knowing he was there meant everything to her. She closed up the garage and left the house through the front door.

He'd gotten out of his car and had opened the passenger door for her. Holden really was the most gorgeous man she'd ever known. She felt his gaze on her with an intensity that sent her pulse fluttering.

"You look lovely tonight."

"Thank you." It would probably shock him if he knew how strong her feelings for him truly were.

As she got inside their arms brushed, stirring her senses.

"How's Chase?"

"He's great and told me he can't wait to be with you again."

"I feel the same way."

They drove to his ranch. When he pulled up in front, she took note of the welcoming wraparound porch. He turned off the engine, and she climbed out before he could open her door.

They weren't on a real date. He'd brought her here so they could talk about the case. She couldn't forget for a minute that she was in the company of the sheriff of Sublette County, who just happened to be the most gorgeous man this side of the Continental Divide.

"If you don't mind, we'll eat in the kitchen. I got off work early so I could make us dinner. All I have to do is grill the steaks. Everything else is ready."

His home had a very clean, modern feel. No frills. She liked it. "What can I do to help?"

"Just sit at the table and enjoy some lemonade."

Before long, they were eating rolls and a green salad along with the steak and baked potatoes he'd made. "This is absolutely delicious, Holden," she said.

"Thanks. It tastes good to me, too."

All the while they ate, she sensed he was building up to tell her something important. When she thought she couldn't stand the suspense any longer, he put down his empty coffee cup and said, "I finally have the proof I've been looking for to arrest Seth Lunt."

She gasped quietly. "You're absolutely sure?"

He nodded. "First, let me show you these blown-up photos from the surveillance tapes." He reached for them on the counter so she could see.

Jessica studied them. The long hair was unmistakable. "That's Seth all right. He had no idea he was being filmed."

"Obviously not. But even more important, he left a three-quarter thumbprint on the Duralast ball joint he put on your car. However, before I could determine it was his print, I had to go to Judge Jenkins. He gave me another search warrant to see the sheets of fingerprints collected by the South Mall dealership where he formerly worked.

"For some miraculous reason, that company required drug tests and fingerprint testing of all their employees. At that point, I called Cyril and asked him to check everything. It was probably too much to hope that Seth's prints would match the ball joint print. Today, Cyril told me to drop by at noon and he'd have answers for me."

Jessica looked at the pictures again, then at him. "Seth couldn't have had any idea that the investigating officer at the accident scene had taken the Duralast ball joint for evidence."

"No, and it was a miracle it was still in the evidence room now. He'd thought he'd gotten away with his crime, not realizing he'd left a fingerprint on it."

Elation swept through Jessica.

"By the way, the cashier's check had two sets of prints, but neither set matched the ones from the ball joint or Seth's personnel file because Bryan wasn't the criminal.

"When I got to forensics there was a gleam in Cyril's eyes. He took me into the lab and said, 'I always knew you were a damn good investigator, but this time you've done something truly remarkable. Come over to the counter and let me show you what you've turned up.'

"I got excited as he laid out the two sets of prints for me and said, 'Here's a picture of the three-quarter thumbprint. Now, take a look at the print you sent from the South Mall dealership. They're a match! Both belong to Seth Lunt!'"

She trembled. "Oh, Holden."

"Your nightmare is about to be over."

Jessica shook her head. "I just can't believe it. You're a genius."

"It doesn't take genius, just perseverance. I asked Cyril if the match with the three-quarter thumbprint would hold up in court because it wasn't a whole print.

He said he'd swear to it for many reasons, and explained why.

"He considers the point system of similarities, but also looks at the ridge width, shape, edge contour and pore distribution. He handed me the magnifying glass so I could see for myself. They looked the same to me compared to the other set of prints.

"Cyril said other experts could try, but they would have a hard time disproving this result on the three-quarter print. Jessica, this gave me enough ammunition to take to the judge for an arrest warrant. We've got him."

She picked up the picture of Seth leaving the dealership. "There he is—going out to the parking lot to do his evil." Tears stung her eyes, but they didn't fall as she stared at Holden. "Because of you, he'll be locked away where he belongs. Thank God for you!" she cried and, in the next moment, buried her face in her hands.

Chapter 8

Holden could see her shoulders shaking and knew what this news meant to her. He came close to losing the battle and just taking her in his arms.

A few minutes later she stirred. "What's going to happen now?"

Holden sucked in his breath. "I've already made plans for him," he said, emotion behind his words.

Her head reared. She wiped the tears off her white cheeks. "So he hid inside the building until he was sure everyone was gone before he went out to sabotage our car. Seth is evil."

"There's no question the judge will say he was cold and calculating. I had those portions of the tapes enlarged and photos taken. It's all part of the evidence I gave the judge for the arrest warrant."

She moaned. "I just can't believe what he did. All

this time I've been cutting his hair while he pretended to be a friend. *He killed Trent!*"

Holden's heart went out to her for the pain she was having to relive. "He'll be charged with first-degree murder. Though Seth didn't know Trent would get in an accident and die, the crime he committed was willful, deliberate and premeditated. He'll go to prison for it."

Jessica examined his rugged features. "To think you caught him at last. You're phenomenal." Her voice shook. "No wonder you were elected sheriff. I'm in awe of you, Holden, and so grateful you've discovered what he did. I can never repay you enough."

"You played a part in this, too," he stated. "If you hadn't noticed that box of used ball joints, Seth would never have had to pay for his crime."

She shook her head. "Don't give me credit. I would have seen them much sooner if I hadn't waited two years before cleaning the garage. Even then, I feel that someone was watching over me when I opened that box because it reminded me of the accident."

"A higher power maybe?"

"Yes. You were so wonderful to see me when I went to your office that day. Your taking me seriously helped reassure me so much."

He covered her hand with his, unable to help it. "Let's be thankful we were able to stop him from committing another crime."

Her brow furrowed. "What do you mean?"

"I have no doubt in my mind he's been waiting to have his chance with you for years. If you had eventually accepted a date with him without knowing what we know now, I'm not sure he wouldn't have kidnapped you."

"Kidnapped?"

"He fits the profile of a real psychopath. That's why he's under police surveillance as we speak. Once he's arrested and taken to jail to be booked, I'll be able to search his property, particularly his van, to see if my instincts bear out my theory.

"Think about it. Seth has already made the phone call to get you to go out with him. This man doesn't leave anything to chance. He's after you, but I'm going to arrest him before he gets the opportunity to make another move."

"W-what are you going to do?" she stammered.

"Before you pick up Chase, we're going to drive to the salon. I'd like you to call your mother and alert her we're on our way there now. Tell her everything that's happened. She has to be a part of what we do to set things up.

"Ask her to start phoning clients tonight to cancel all the appointments for tomorrow. When we get to the salon, I want you to call Seth on the salon phone and say that you'll go out with him tomorrow evening after work at six."

She cringed. "What if he changes his mind for some reason and wants to go out another night?"

"Then you'll play along. If he doesn't answer, then leave the message on his voice mail and give him your cell phone number. That way he can reach you no matter where you are. But my impression is that he can't wait to be with you and will jump at the chance when you tell him yes."

Jessica shook her head. "I've seen enough news about stalkers to know they're out there, but you never think it will happen to you."

"Seth has been extremely clever to have waited two years. His pretense of being a friend to you and Chase is classic. That's a long time for him to have planned and prepared for this moment. He's methodical and made certain to leave enough time since the accident before carrying out his dream of getting you for himself. He may even have seen you with me."

"It's terrifying to think he's been targeting me all this time."

"Thankfully we still have the opportunity to stop him permanently."

"I'm nervous."

"Anyone would be, but be assured that as of tonight, you, Chase and your mother are under police protection. It's all been arranged with the chief of police. Deputies have been assigned to keep you safe. They're outside the salon now."

"You're kidding! And they'll be watching my house tonight?"

"Yours, and they'll also be protecting Wilma's. You'll need to call her when we get to the salon and tell her what's happening. I'll want her address and phone number. It's possible Seth might show up at the salon tomorrow with a devious plan once you've called him."

"But he doesn't know where Wilma lives."

"I think he knows every move you make."

A cry came out of her. "If he ever hurt Chase… Oh, Holden, this is all so unreal."

"Don't worry, Seth won't get near any of you. Tomorrow you'll drive over to the salon with Chase and park where you always do. A police van will be waiting in back to take you, your son and your mom to the Whitebark Hotel where you'll be given a room with TV, room service and constant police surveillance. When the arrest is made, you'll be driven back to the salon to get your car."

She took a shuddering breath. "What will I tell Chase?"

"Leave that to me after we pick him up."

She bowed her head. "You'll be making the arrest at the salon?"

"That's right. The open sign will be displayed in the window. I'll be hiding inside while the undercover officers surround the shop. When he drives up in his white 2017 RAM ProMaster and walks in, he'll be in for the surprise of his life.

"To be on the safe side, it wouldn't be out of character for him to show up earlier than six, so we've got two undercover female officers who are going to pose as a client and beautician. They'll also be on hand to supply more backup."

He squeezed her hand a little tighter while she came to grips with what he'd just told her. "Don't you know that I'd never let anyone harm you?"

"I do know that," she said. "His arrest can't come soon enough for me."

"You took the words right out of my mouth. I do this for a living, and believe me, I'm invested in this case. You have no idea how much I'm looking forward to taking this guy down personally. Come on. Let's get to the salon."

They hurried out to his car. He started the engine and they left. En route, Jessica called her mom using the speakerphone so he could hear them. She told her everything, including the specific plans for tomorrow.

A strange sound came out of her mother. "Seth

couldn't have been nicer when he gave Chase that truck the other day. He always spoke so highly of Trent. Nothing in his demeanor has ever given him away. It's beyond comprehension."

"Tell me about it. He personifies the meaning of sinister."

Her mother showed incredible calm once she got over the shock of learning that Seth was a criminal.

"That sheriff of yours is brilliant, a man in a billion."

Jessica flashed him a look that turned his heart over. "Don't you think I know that?"

Her mom actually chuckled. "Yes, darling. I saw and heard it the moment you told me what happened after you came back from his office that first day."

Suddenly the speakerphone went off. "We'll be there in a minute, Mom."

Holden savored their conversation all the way to the salon. He nodded to the undercover officers stationed on the street in front of Style Clips where other cars were parked.

Jessica got out of his car and they went inside the shop through the front door. She called to her mother who said she'd be right down, then made the call to Wilma.

Once that was accomplished he watched and waited while Jessica walked over to the counter and made the phone call using the salon phone to Seth. She put it on speaker so Holden could hear. To his satisfaction, the suspect answered on the third ring.

"Well, what do you know?" The tone of Seth's voice grated on Holden.

"This is the first chance I've had to return your call."

"You sound in a better mood than when you were at the dealership, Jess."

Jess?

He saw her hand tighten on the receiver. Had he ever called her that before?

"That's because I was hoping for a little higher offer on the truck. But in the end, I sold it to Bryan. Now I have more room in my garage."

"I would have made an offer, but I knew Bryan really wanted it so I backed off."

Holden knew that had to be a lie. Seth didn't need a used truck. He was living pretty off his father's money.

"I'm just glad it's settled and we're both happy. I now have a new Toyota."

"When I take you home after dinner tomorrow night, I'd like to see it. By the way, how do you feel about Italian?"

"That sounds good to me." Her eyes focused on Holden. "Chase loves spaghetti and meatballs. Thank you for the invitation. I've got to go."

"Hold on. Don't be in such a hurry to get off."

Seth's temper was already giving him away.

"Sorry. Chase is waiting. Was there something else you needed to say?"

"Yeah. I'm glad you called me back. I wasn't sure you would."

"Why not? All you guys at the dealership have been so good to me over the past couple years." Holden could tell she'd said that through clenched teeth.

"But I didn't know if you were willing to go out with another man."

"Like I said, you've been a friend to me and Chase."

Jessica had done some fast thinking to answer him that way.

"I guess friends is as good a way to start as any," he drawled.

Seth was so tied up in knots talking to her, he wasn't being careful.

"I'm sorry, but I have to start getting Chase ready for bed. See you tomorrow after work."

"Shall I come to the front or back door of the salon?"

With that question Jessica had to know he'd been stalking her. She doubted that any of her clients knew she used the back door. She lost a little color. "The front is fine."

After she hung up, her beautiful green eyes—darkened by fear—met Holden's. "He's driven by here and probably followed me home many times. He's got me terrified."

"You may be reeling, but you handled that call like a pro. I know how hard it was on you. You were very courageous considering who was on the other end of that phone. Just remember that tomorrow night he'll be put out of commission on a permanent basis and you'll never have to talk to him again." He cocked his head. "Tell me something. Has he ever called you Jess before?"

"Never."

His lips twisted. "After waiting for so long, he thinks he's finally gotten the green light with you."

Jessica's mother stood nearby. "Sheriff Granger?"

He turned to her. "Please, call me Holden."

Jessica made the introductions. "This is my mother, Erica Harrison Stevens."

"It's a pleasure to meet you, Mrs. Stevens."

"I've been so anxious to meet you and thank you," Erica spoke up. "Per your instructions I've canceled every appointment for tomorrow, and have told my other employees to take the day off."

"You'll all be reimbursed."

"That won't be necessary. I'm still trying to find a way to repay you for finding out what really happened when Trent took that car for a test run. And now you're saving Jessica's life." Gratitude filled her eyes and voice before she reached out to hug him.

Holden could have told the charming woman that all the payment he wanted was to go on seeing her daughter in the nonprofessional sense. If he were being honest, he couldn't think about anything else. His attraction to Jessica had been worrying him from the beginning and had played havoc with his guilt. When Cynthia died, he'd thought he'd buried his heart with her.

"I'm more anxious than you to rid this world of the man who brought such pain to your lives." He looked at Jessica. "If you're ready, we'll go pick up Chase and drive you home."

She nodded and gave her mother a long, hard hug. "See you in the morning at the usual time. Just so you know, undercover officers are out in front and will stay there all night."

"That's good to know. Thank you, Holden."

"Your safety is everything."

Holden walked Jessica out to his car and she gave him directions to Donna's house. When they pulled into the Sillses' driveway, he spotted the officers parked across the street in an unmarked car and pointed them out to her.

"They'll follow us to your house."

She stared at him for a minute. "What if I had never come to your office? I can't think about it or I get deathly sick."

"Then stop thinking."

"You're right. It's getting late. I'll run in and get Chase."

"I have two car seats and put one in the back for him. I use them when I drive to Cody to see the family. I'm planning on getting away soon. After this whole business is over, I'd like to take you and Chase with me."

"I can't imagine anything more wonderful than going on a little vacation with you. Chase would be in heaven. I'm sure I can arrange it. Millie and I trade off at work when something important comes up."

"Then we'll plan on it." Until he'd met Jessica, he'd never dreamed of taking a woman home to meet his family.

She got out of the car and hurried to the front door. He walked around to open the back door of the car for Chase. The cute kid rushed out ahead of her and ran to him. "Holden!" he cried and gave him a big hug.

Holden picked him up, liking the feel of Chase's arms clinging to him. This boy had become precious to him in more ways than one. "It's good to see you, too."

The three of them chatted all the way to her house where he pulled into the driveway. After he stopped the car, he turned to Chase, who sat behind Jessica.

"I have a little surprise for you. In the morning you're going to go stay at the Whitebark Hotel with your mom and your nana for the day."

He undid his seat belt. "How come?"

"Because tomorrow I have to arrest a really bad guy. While I look for him, I want the three of you kept safe so I can do my job as sheriff. If I had to worry about you, I wouldn't be able to concentrate. Can I commission Wolverine to wear the sheriff's hat and protect your family until it's over?"

Chase's face lit up in a huge smile. "Sure, I'll do it!"

Holden's heart melted. "I knew I could count on you. It'll be fun with lots of food and TV to watch. They also have an indoor pool and a gym so you'd better pack your swimsuit."

"Will you come and swim with us after you've caught him?"

"Maybe. But if it's too late, I'll come by your house tomorrow night after you're home."

"Are you scared?"

"Nope. This is one criminal I can't wait to catch."

"When I grow up I'm going to be a sheriff just like you!"

Holden saw tears in Jessica's eyes, but didn't quite know what they meant. He was struggling to blink back his own. To have a son like Chase...

"You're already on your way. I'll walk you up to the house. It's getting late and we all have to be up early tomorrow to do our jobs."

"Yup. Come on, Mom."

Jessica flashed Holden a smile that thanked him for handling what could have been a difficult moment.

Chase opened the door and got out. Jessica followed suit and hurried up to the front door of the house with her son. She unlocked it, then turned to Holden. "I know you have to go. Please call me tomorrow when you get a minute."

Her green eyes implored him. "In case you didn't know, that's the first thing on my agenda. Don't hesitate to call me if something alarms you, even if it's the middle of the night." If they'd been alone, he'd have pulled her against his body and shown her exactly what she meant to him.

Jessica clung to his arm. "This is it then, until it's over tomorrow night."

He sucked in his breath. "It *will* be over. Don't doubt me on that."

"I could never doubt you," she whispered.

"See ya, Holden."

Holden got down on his haunches. "We'll be together tomorrow night, bud." *I swear it*, he vowed as the two of them hugged. Before emotions kept him there any longer, he tousled Chase's dark blond head and rushed back to the car.

Sleep came to Jessica only for a few hours. Fear for Holden's safety while he faced Seth drove her from the bed at six on Tuesday morning. She slipped out to the barn to take Bucky for a ride. After making sure he had plenty of food and water, she left him in the pasture and rushed inside to fix breakfast.

Her son came bouncing into the kitchen to eat, wearing his sheriff hat. The other day she'd pinned it in the back to make it tighter so it wouldn't fall off. He'd dressed in his shorts and another emoji T-shirt. In one bag, he carried his plastic building blocks and blaster gun. The other small bag he carried held his bathing suit and goggles.

He wolfed down his food he was so excited. "How soon are we going to Nana's?"

"The second we finish eating."

"Did you pack your swimsuit, too?"

"Yes, darling."

"How long do you think it will take Holden to catch that bad guy?"

Her concern for the man she'd fallen in love with had increased her heart rate to a dangerous level. "I don't know, but if you remember, he told us it would all be over tonight."

"He's not scared of anything. Does he have a son like me?"

The fork slipped from her fingers and clattered on the table. "No. His wife died before they could have children."

"She did?" Jessica could hear Chase's mind working.

Ever since she'd been given the early menopause diagnosis, Jessica had been living with pain because she could never give birth to another child. Which meant she could never have another man's baby if by some miracle she married again.

"It made him very sad and he moved here from Cody a few years ago in order to become the chief of police."

"But he's the sheriff!"

"Not at first. After he'd lived here awhile, then he was elected sheriff."

"That's because he's so brave, huh?"

"It's just one of the great things about him."

"I want to be a sheriff when I grow up. I love him."

Oh, Chase...

A while ago he'd told her he wanted to be a mechanic like Trent when he grew up. Now his hero worship of Holden was off the charts. So was Jessica's. She got out of the chair to clear the table and clean up the kitchen.

"I think we're ready," she finally announced, having already packed some personal items and her bathing suit.

Together they went out to the car through the garage and left the house. She could breathe more easily knowing the police officers were out there and would follow them to the salon.

When she pulled around the back of the shop ten minutes later and parked the car, she saw her mother standing there with two undercover officers. The second she turned off the engine, Chase got out with his stuff and ran toward his nana. Jessica followed and hugged both of them before they were ushered into a van.

Once they reached the hotel and were taken up to their room via the freight elevator, Jessica's cell phone rang. She felt a sense of dread. *What if it was Seth?*

While Chase ran around checking out the room, she exchanged a worried glance with her mom before looking at the caller ID. The relief of knowing who was on the other end sent her into the bedroom for privacy.

"Holden?" She was out of breath with excitement to hear his voice.

"I only have a second. The deputy guarding your hotel room let me know you're all there safe and sound. Now I can do what I have to."

"Please don't let anything happen to you. I—"

"Got to go. See you tonight."

It was a good thing he'd cut her off before she had

the chance to pour out her love for him. Though he'd continue to say it was his job to rid the world of criminals, he was putting his life on the line for her and Chase.

Chapter 9

Holden and two other deputies had been parked in unmarked cars around the outside of the Mid-Valley dealership since following Seth from his condo early that morning. He could have arrested him there, but in case he'd seen Holden with Jessica and figured something was going on, Holden wanted to catch him off guard. No one could get inside that unstable mind of his or know what he was planning. Holden needed to be prepared for the unexpected.

At ten after one in the afternoon, he watched Seth leave the building and go out to the east parking lot for his truck. He could be on a lunch break. But as Holden and the deputies followed him to his upscale condo on the other side of town where he disappeared inside, it was clear he'd left work for the day.

This new complex had been built only eight months

ago. Seth's well-to-do attorney father who did business all over the state had to be footing the bill. How else could his service writer son afford to live here and drive the Lexus he could see as Seth pulled into the two-car garage?

An hour later he left in his truck and drove to Jessica's house. *Holden knew it!* The paranoid stalker wanted to see if she'd stayed home instead of going to work. Was he worried she was trying to avoid him?

Seth wasn't leaving anything to chance. Holden broke out in a cold sweat as he imagined what Seth had been planning. He had no doubt he carried a weapon, maybe more than one.

After telling the deputies to watch Seth's every move, Holden sped away and headed for the hair salon. Five minutes later he heard from Deputy Green out at her house.

"What's happening, Rick?"

"The suspect went to the front door of her house. When there was no answer, he walked around the back and knocked on that door for a while. Then he looked in the windows, but they're all shuttered. We have it on tape."

Holden's eyes closed tightly for a minute. It was terrifying to think what was going on in Seth's brain. The tape would provide more evidence to add a stalking charge.

"Where is he now?"

"He just got back in his truck and we're following him."

"Keep me posted."

He nodded to the deputies already set up outside and

in back of Style Clips. Once he'd parked his car across the street, he entered the salon.

"Sheriff," the three undercover female officers greeted him. One of them looked like she was getting her hair frosted. Another held a brush. Deputy Otterson stood at the desk. No one walking in would know what was really going on.

"We'll be having a visitor soon. He's dangerous."

"We're ready, sir."

"You know the drill. When the suspect walks in, tell him Jessica is in the back room, but she'll be out in a minute."

Holden knew it was the place where they mixed the ingredients for hair color. He walked back and hid himself behind the door. With it left partially open, he could see the salon interior. Before long he got a call from Rick, the deputy following Seth in a van with Deputy Jose Romero.

"He just parked near the salon and is getting out of his truck."

"Good work. Be ready to close in."

No sooner had he clicked off than Seth entered the shop. Seth had changed out of his work uniform and wore a short-sleeved shirt and jeans.

"Hi!" Deputy Otterson spoke to him. "I haven't seen you here before. Do you want a haircut? If so, you'll have to wait about five minutes."

"I'm here to see Jessica."

"Oh. You must be the man she's going out to dinner with. But I thought she said you were leaving at the end of the day."

"We are, but I came by to talk to her for a minute."

"She's in the back mixing a color, but she'll be right out. Do you want a soda while you wait?"

Adrenaline surged through Holden as he watched Seth stand there, looking around. He could tell the guy was trying to decide what to do next.

Without giving her an answer he said, "Maybe I'll just walk back there." The man was out of control.

The deputy had to think fast. "I guess that'll be all right."

Holden backed against the wall as Seth started toward the room. "Jess?" he called out and rapped on the door before coming all the way in.

At that moment Holden tripped Seth so his legs went out from under him and he fell to the floor facedown. A surprised cry rang out before he started spouting venom and tried to get up. But though he struggled violently, Holden held him pinned and was able to cuff him.

By now the three male deputies appeared. One of them searched him for weapons and retrieved a Glock revolver and a knife. The other two pulled Seth to his feet and secured him while Holden read him his Miranda rights. The man's eyes were dark slits of rage.

"Seth Morten Lunt, you're under arrest for the murder of Trent Fleming. You have the right to remain silent. Anything you say can and will be used against you in a court of law. You have the right to an attorney. If you can't afford one, one will be appointed to you. Do you understand the rights I've just read to you?"

Seth spit at him, but it just missed Holden and ran down Seth's shirt.

"Take him out to the van."

"What murder? You can't do this to me!" he shouted

as they dragged him through the shop. "Do you know who I am? My father's going to hear about this!" he snarled. "You'll never get away with it!"

Once he was taken outside and put in the van, Holden pulled Deputy Green aside. "Get the keys to his truck and drive it in. I want to take a look at the interior after I see him booked."

"Yes, sir."

"It's been nice working with you. Your superior is going to hear about your outstanding service."

"Thank you, sir."

Holden shook the hands of the female deputies. "You made this the perfect setup in what could have been a lethal situation. Our suspect had a wild look when he came in, but you handled it like the pros you are. Your bravery in the line of fire is commendable. This case was particularly important to me. I'm recommending all three of you for promotions."

"Thank you, Sheriff Granger."

"Thank *you*. You're free to leave and go back to the police station to report to Chief Wayland."

He followed them out the door and locked it before walking across the street to his car. The next order of business was to drive to the jail and make sure Seth was booked properly. When he'd seen the process through, he would phone Jessica and tell her the good news.

Right now it was hard to believe he'd caught Seth and had made it impossible for him to ever hurt Jessica or anyone else again.

Seth's eyes glittered with hatred when Holden entered the room and watched him being fingerprinted and photographed. Once he was hauled to his cell where he'd be kept overnight before his arraignment in the morning, Holden walked to another part of the facility to take a good look inside Seth's truck.

"Sheriff—" Rick Green called to him. "You've got to see what we've found. My partner, Jose, is with me."

Holden feared that looking inside would give him nightmares, but he had to do a search to write up his report. The two doors at the back were opened to show a single bed, chains, duct tape, a camera and arm and leg restraints. Beyond the bed were boxes of food and bottles of water.

He'd seen sights like this before, but knowing this was all meant for Jessica turned his blood cold. When he looked inside the glove compartment, he found a map of the Wind River Mountains. Seth had used a magic marker to highlight isolated areas where he'd planned to take her.

It took an hour to log everything in while the forensics group took over. With this amount of evidence, Seth would be put away for life. But Holden still wasn't through and left with Deputies Green and Romero to search Seth's condo.

He needed one more piece of evidence to link everything and found it when he discovered pictures of Jessica on the walls and bathroom mirror. Many of them had been taken when she was a teenager.

With everything recorded and photographed, they drove back to headquarters. It was 6:50 p.m. when Holden checked in with Walt. "The arrest has been made and I'm leaving to take care of some personal business. Phone me if you need me. Otherwise I'll be at the Lunt arraignment in the morning before coming in to the office."

Exhausted physically and emotionally, Holden drove

home and took a long hot shower. But nothing could wash away the horror of what he'd seen. After shaving, he pulled on his black swimming trunks. Chase was waiting to play in the pool with him and Holden didn't want to disappoint him.

After dressing in jeans and a casual shirt, he left in his Subaru for the hotel. On the drive over, he phoned Jessica.

"Holden—" She picked up after the first ring. "At last," she said. "Are you all right?"

Hearing her voice changed his whole mood. "It's over. Seth is in jail at this very moment and awaiting arraignment with the judge in the morning."

"Oh, thank you. Thank you!" She broke down. He had to wait a moment until her sobs subsided. "Where are you? I have to see you."

She didn't know the half of it. "I'm on my way to the hotel. Get your bathing suits on and I'll meet you at the swimming pool."

"You don't have to do that. Not after what you've been through. Have you even eaten?"

"Not yet."

"Then I'll have a meal brought out to the pool for you."

"You don't need to bother."

"How can you say that after what you've done?"

"There's a lot I have to tell you, Jessica."

"After we go to my house and I put Chase to bed, I want to hear everything." No, she didn't. He would never tell her all of it. "My son is going to be overjoyed when I tell him you're on your way. Right now he's in the other room watching the Cartoon Network. He's been driving us crazy waiting for you to call."

"I couldn't come any sooner."

"I know that—believe me, I'm not complaining. The fact that you're alive means my prayers have been answered. Holden? Are you really all right? Don't pretend with me."

"I've never been better in my life. That psychopath will never hurt anyone again. You and Chase are safe. Don't you know that's the most important thing in the world to me? Nothing else matters."

"I feel the same way about you. I've been in agony." Her voice throbbed. "How far away are you?"

How he loved this woman! "I'm almost at the hotel."

"Then I'll get off the phone this instant and order your dinner. See you in a few minutes. Please don't get into an accident before you get here!"

Holden laughed out loud. Just talking to her like this made those nightmare images disappear into the furthest recesses of his psyche.

Jessica got in the pool with Chase while they waited for him.

"Holden!"

Her son climbed out of the water and ran toward his hero as Holden walked out from the changing room.

"Did you catch the bad guy?"

"You bet I did."

"Hooray!"

Her eyes feasted on the tall, gorgeous man clad in black trunks. He swept her son up in his arms.

"I was afraid you couldn't come."

"Hey—I told you I'd be over. Shall we jump in together, or shall I go in first and you jump to me?"

"I'll jump to you."

Holden put him down and jumped in. He came up right by Jessica. The way those silvery eyes looked at her, she couldn't catch her breath.

"You don't know how long I've been waiting for this," Holden said.

Before she could get out a single word, he turned to Chase standing on the edge of the pool. "Okay. It's your turn. One, two, three!"

Her normally timid son whom you couldn't bribe to get on a horse, jumped in without hesitation. Holden brought him to the surface. "That was terrific."

Chase clung to his neck with a huge smile. "Did you see that, Nana?"

"You were wonderful!" Jessica's mother called out. She was sitting at one of the tables fully dressed.

"Will you pull me around the pool? I'm going to take swimming lessons this summer."

"That's a great idea. I took lessons at your age, too. Come on." He took off with Chase who was having the time of his life. While they were circling the pool for the third time, a waiter brought Holden's dinner out to the table.

She reached for Chase. "Come on, honey. We'll practice holding our breath while the sheriff eats." She darted Holden a glance. "I ordered prime rib and all the trimmings for you."

"How lucky can a man get?" he murmured in his deep voice. It filled her with excitement as he heaved himself to the edge and got out. She was glad he could talk to her mother in private for a few minutes. Jessica would get him to herself later when they were alone.

After playing with Chase for a while longer, they

got out and she put on her beach robe. "We're going up to the room to change our clothes."

Holden had been watching her. It seemed like every time she felt his eyes on her, her legs started to tremble. "Meet me in the foyer in fifteen minutes and I'll drive you all home."

"Yay!" Chase ran ahead of her and beat her to the room. There was no more police presence. Nothing could have made her happier.

Jessica showered and washed her hair fast. The smell of chlorine bothered her too much not to be fresh. When they dressed and met Holden and her mother at the entrance, Jessica's hair was still damp with no style whatsoever, but she didn't care.

Holden led them out to his car and drove them to the back entrance of the salon. Jessica noticed her car was gone.

"Some of the deputies returned your car to your house."

Amazing. Holden thought of everything.

She walked her mother inside and up the stairs to make certain everything was all right.

"Holden told me what went on, honey. He's an incredible man."

"Oh, Mom, words can't describe what I'm feeling right now."

"I know. I can see how you feel. Tonight you can go home and put your worries behind you."

She nodded. "See you in the morning."

Jessica hurried back to the car where her son and Holden were deep in conversation about a new Aquaman movie that was coming out soon. "They say his skin is so thick he can handle the pressures in the deepest depths of the ocean."

"Can he talk to fish?"

"I don't think so. But I read that he feels the tides of the ocean like fish and sometimes swims with them."

"Will you take me to see it when it comes, Holden?"

He flicked Jessica a warm side-glance. "That's up to your mother."

"She'll probably say it's too scary."

"I probably will," Jessica said, "but we'll see."

Holden chuckled.

"Could we go for a hike this weekend?"

"Maybe. I have a lot of work and will have to see."

A sigh escaped her son. "I wish you didn't have to work." Out of the mouths of babes. That was exactly how she felt.

"Guess what?"

"What?"

"How would you and your mom like to drive to Cody with me and Blackie pretty soon?"

"You're taking your horse?"

"Yes. He needs a vacation, too. Think how bored he gets just going out to the pasture every day by himself. I bet Bucky gets bored. He could come with us, and maybe even Sparky."

"Mom? Could we? Please…"

"I'm ready for a vacation. I think it sounds terrific."

"Then it's settled," Holden said. "I want to visit my family. We'll stay at my parents' ranch house, and my niece and nephew will come over to play. You'll like Chrissy. I've told you about her. You'll like Rob, too. He's eight years old. She loves superhero movies and got a superhero costume for her birthday she wears a lot."

"Did she get to watch that movie?"

"I don't know. It's an old one. I'll have to ask my sister when we get there."

"Nana gave me a superhero wolf costume for Halloween."

"Lucky you. Why don't you bring it with you if you come to Cody?"

"I can't wait!"

They'd just pulled in the driveway. Chase got out first and carried his things to the front door. Jessica followed with her overnight bag and let them in the house.

"It's getting late, Chase. Since you've been swimming, we'll skip your bath and get you in your pajamas."

"I wish I didn't have to go to bed yet."

"I know."

"Good night, Holden."

"It is now." Holden gave him a hug. "Get a good sleep, Chase, and I'll see you sometime this coming weekend."

Jessica turned to him. "Please make yourself comfortable. You're welcome to fix coffee. I'll be back soon."

"Take your time. I have some phone calls to make."

Jessica went to Chase's bedroom with him. Once he'd said his prayers and climbed under the covers, he looked up at Jessica. "I'm so glad he caught that bad guy."

"So am I."

"I love him, Mom," he said in a thoughtful voice.

She knew her son loved them both. "I love you, too."

When she returned to the living room ten minutes

later, Holden was no longer on the phone. She sank down on the end of the couch opposite the chair where he was sitting.

"Tell me everything that happened," she urged him.

"Ten deputies were involved, covering all the places Seth might go. This morning I followed him from his work to his condo. Then he went to your house before going to the salon."

Her eyes closed tightly. "He came to my house today?"

"Around two. He cased your home outside to make sure you weren't avoiding him. If you'd been there, it was possible he might have forced you into his van. He was carrying a gun and knife when I arrested him."

She put a hand to her mouth in horror.

"I went to your mother's shop where the female deputies were stationed. Seth showed up there around three and said he wanted to talk to you. They told him you were in the back room where I was hiding. He came looking for you. I tripped him and he fell. That gave me the chance to cuff him. It was all over just that fast."

A groan came out of her. "I'm sure there was a lot more to it than that."

"Not really," he lied. She didn't need to know the rest. "We can thank Providence he had no idea what was waiting for him. I read him his rights and the deputies took him to jail where he was booked. Tomorrow morning he'll be arraigned before the judge who's been helping me with the warrants."

"You solved this case so fast. How am I ever going to repay you?" Tears trickled down her cheeks. "I know I keep saying it, but it's true. What if you hadn't moved here from Cody? Trent's crime would never have been uncovered. You're so amazing…no one else can hold a candle to you."

Holden scoffed. "That's nice to hear, but don't forget I had motivation. That crime was committed while I was the police chief. It meant I had unfinished business to take care."

"I've been so blessed. Do you think it would be possible to talk to the officer who investigated Trent's crash? He was the one who discovered the loose ball joint and sent it in for evidence. Without it, you wouldn't have found Seth's thumbprint."

"That's true."

"I want to thank him personally."

"Because he followed protocol, it made it possible for me to conduct my investigation. I've wanted to talk to him myself. We can do it together. When I get back to the office I'll look in the files for his number and—"

Suddenly Holden's phone rang, interrupting him. His work was never done. After this arrest she could only imagine how many loose ends he needed to tie up. While he finished talking, she went out to the kitchen.

But before she could start making the coffee, he came in with a sober look on his face. "I have to go out on an emergency, but I'll call you in the morning after the arraignment. We still have so much to talk about."

She nodded and followed him to the front door. He raced out to his car. But when she got in bed, something was haunting her. Holden held her heart, but she had no right to it. No right to impossible dreams of being his wife, even if he had feelings for her. What on earth was she thinking? She knew how much he loved children and she couldn't have another baby— let alone Holden's.

* * *

"All rise. The Sublette County District Court of Wyoming is now in session. The Honorable Judge Harold Garson is presiding."

Where in the hell was Judge Jenkins?

Holden stood at the back of the courtroom, not liking this at all. He'd arrived at the courthouse early to give his report with all the evidence to Russ Doyle, the prosecuting attorney. Why had this happened?

He ground his teeth as eight handcuffed prisoners were brought in from the jail dressed in the same blue jumpsuits, no matter the degree of their crimes. It had been a busy twenty-four hours for the officers since they'd brought in this many prisoners at once.

His gaze focused on Seth, who shot him a malevolent glance as he was brought in. Holden could feel his hatred from across the room. After Seth's ten-year plan that had already included murder, Holden had been the one to thwart Seth at the very moment he was about to kidnap Jessica.

Two men looking like well-dressed Wall Street attorneys followed Seth. The shorter one shared a certain resemblance in body shape and height to Seth. That must be Seth's father. But Seth reminded Holden of an unkempt miscreant. His father nudged his son, who finally shuffled the rest of the way in and was told to sit down. Then the two men took seats behind him.

There could be no greater satisfaction for Holden than to see Seth answer to his crimes before the judge and be incarcerated.

The arraignment got underway. Holden sat there, waiting anxiously with the other officers for this to be over. It was almost one o'clock before Seth's name was called last. The judge called on him to stand and acknowledge his identity.

"Seth Morten Lunt."

"The court understands the defendant has availed himself of private counsel."

"Yes, your Honor. I'm William Margets, criminal attorney from the law firm of Margets and Thiesen in Jackson Hole, Wyoming. I'll be representing him."

Holden grimaced. Seth's dad had called in a big gun.

"Has the defense attorney read the police report and complaint to the defendant?"

"Yes, your Honor."

"The defendant has been arrested for first-degree murder. How does the defendant plea?"

"Not guilty."

That was no surprise to Holden. Not guilty was the usual answer.

"So entered. The defendant will be remanded to the custody of his parents tomorrow morning, and will remain under house arrest with an ankle monitor until his trial scheduled for July 7. Bail is set at $1,000,000."

"It has been paid, your Honor."

What?

Holden felt as if a shell had exploded in his gut. Had Judge Jenkins been bought? Seth was a cold-blooded killer. This was a mistake with horrendous consequences if he escaped.

The judge pounded the gavel again. "Court is adjourned."

Seth got up from the chair and sent Holden a mocking smile before being taken back to his cell.

Holden shot out of the courtroom and rushed back

to his office. "Walt? I've got to leave for a few hours. Will you cover for me?"

"Sure," the other man said without asking any questions.

"Thanks."

With the judge's pronouncement, another nightmare was starting and Jessica needed to be warned ASAP!

Chapter 10

Jessica hadn't slept all night. She had hoped Holden would have called her by now. It was a miracle she was still standing at one in the afternoon, finishing a client's haircut. Millie was the only one in the shop with her because her mother had gone to the dentist and it was Dottie's day off.

After the client paid her at the front counter and they were alone, Millie walked over to Jessica. "Are you expecting the sheriff?"

Jessica, who'd just started sweeping the hair off the floor, reeled in place. "What are you talking about?"

"I saw his truck pull into a parking space out front."

Her heart leaped to her throat. *Holden?* What was he doing here while she was working? He'd been to the arraignment earlier today, and she'd supposed he was still at headquarters. She heard the little bell that sounded when someone entered the shop.

"Good morning, ladies." His deep, rich voice penetrated her body.

"Sheriff—" Millie acknowledged him. "Are you here for a haircut?" she teased.

"Not today. I came to see Mrs. Fleming when she's not busy."

Jessica turned to look at him. He was wearing a new sheriff's cap with his uniform. She hadn't seen him wear it before. He looked so different, like he was a superstar baseball player or something.

"Hi," she said in an unsteady voice. Jessica was so shaken to see him her hands trembled as she put the broom away. *Please let it be good news.* Still trembling, she turned to him.

He gave her a probing stare. "Is there someplace we can go talk for a minute?"

Millie could hear everything. "Why don't you go upstairs? I'll text you when your next appointment comes in."

"Thank you," she whispered before looking at Holden. "Come with me."

He followed her to the door that led to the back of the shop. She was intensely aware of him as he climbed the stairs behind her to the living room of her mother's apartment.

Jessica took a deep breath. "Why are you here? I don't understand. Did you go to Seth's arraignment?"

"Yes. I just came from there." There was no light in his eyes.

She got a sick feeling in the pit of her stomach. "What's wrong? How did the arraignment go?"

"In the one way I'd hoped wouldn't happen."

Her heart plummeted. "Tell me."

"In the first place, Judge Jenkins who knows all about this case, wasn't there to preside. Judge Garson did the honors. When Seth was brought into the courtroom in cuffs, his father and a hotshot criminal attorney from Jackson Hole came in with him.

"After the judge told him why he'd been arrested, his attorney pled not guilty. At that point, Judge Garson remanded Seth to the custody of his parents. He'll be released from jail tomorrow morning."

"No!" Jessica cried out in anguish. "You can't be serious!"

"He'll be under house arrest with an ankle monitor. The judge set the bail at a million dollars, and of course it was paid."

The color left her face. "When is his trial?"

"July 7."

"I don't believe this has happened. I thought you said that first-degree murder didn't allow for bail."

"It doesn't, unless something shady has gone on."

"Holden—this changes everything. He's not behind bars yet and anything could happen."

"I've already arranged for 24/7 surveillance of his parents' home. He won't be able to make a move without us knowing about it."

"But Seth has killed before. He's capable of anything."

"I agree, but I'm not going to let anything happen to you or Chase."

She shook her head. "Why is the trial so far off? I wish it was sooner."

"It's not a long time, actually. Before you know it, he'll be sent to the penitentiary in Rawlins."

"How can you be so sure?"

"You're just going to have to trust me on this." For the first time since they'd been together, he slid his hands to her shoulders, taking her by surprise. She felt their heat beneath her blouse.

The closeness of their bodies caused her heart to thud so hard, he had to feel it. "If he's dangerous, you could be hurt, too, Holden."

His handsome face darkened with lines. "It's you I'm worried about. If anything happened to you because of a miscalculation on my part..." The next thing she knew his head descended and that compelling mouth covered hers.

A moan escaped her throat. There was nothing tentative about the way he deepened their kiss or her need to feel his mouth on hers.

It seemed like an eternity since she'd been held and kissed like this. After Trent's death, she never imagined having these feelings again, or finding a man who could thrill her to the core of her being the way Holden did.

He'd caught her so off guard, she hadn't had time to think about what she was doing. All she knew was that she craved the rush of being in his arms. She wanted it to go on forever and lost track of time. As they came close to devouring each other, she heard the ding on her phone that meant Millie was texting her.

Holden reluctantly relinquished his hold on her and stepped away. She reached for her phone. Your last appointment canceled.

Jessica looked up at him. "I don't have any more clients."

"Even so, it's probably a good thing we were interrupted," he said in a husky tone, sounding out of breath. "I'm sorry, Jessica. I didn't mean for this to happen."

"Neither did I," she whispered.

"I won't lie." His eyes glinted with silver fire. "I've been attracted to you from the time you walked into my office. But I swear that until now, I've never crossed the line in my career with anyone else."

She lifted her head. "I believe you. Just so you know, I haven't been with another man, let alone kissed anyone, since Trent. I enjoyed kissing you, too, but you already know that."

"That doesn't help me." A bleakness had entered his eyes. They were alive with emotion. "Do you mind that I kissed you?"

"Mind?" A slight gasp escaped. "How can you even ask me that? I've been aching for you to hold me." Her last few words were smothered as his lips covered hers again and coherent thought ceased. Nothing held her back as she tried to show him what he meant to her.

Jessica didn't know how long they tried to appease their hunger. She forgot the world while Holden's mouth did the most thrilling things to her.

"I want you so badly it's painful," he whispered against her throat.

"Then you have some idea how I feel," she said softly, running her hands through his hair. "I'll admit it. I've lost my head over you and it's permanent."

He lifted his head and cupped her face in his hands. "I was marking time for three years until you walked into my office. It was a life-changing moment I haven't recovered from. After Cynthia died, I wasn't sure when or if it would ever happen to me. Do you know what I'm telling you?"

"I hope it's what I'm dying to hear you say."

"You mean that I've fallen in love with you? I've been afraid to tell you how I feel about you while I've been investigating this case, but today I can't help myself."

"Oh, Holden, I'm in love with you, too. You know I am, so much so that I can't sleep or eat. It's insane how fast my feelings for you have grown."

"Darling—" He covered her mouth in a kiss that had her reeling with desire. To be in love like this again and have that love reciprocated by the most exciting man in the world was nothing short of heaven on earth. "You're so beautiful, Jessica. I can't believe we didn't meet before now."

"I've been thinking about that, too. Mom said she saw you in the Fourth of July parade last year, but I was sick in bed with the flu. She took Chase with her. I guess I don't have to tell you how my son feels about you."

"That boy has worked his way into my heart. There's a sweetness in him, just like his mother. From the beginning, the thought of your being in danger made me realize just how necessary you are to my existence, but right now I have to go."

"I understand, but first you need to know how crazy in love with you I am. I adore you, Holden." She threw her arms around his neck and kissed every part of his handsome face.

The warmth and safety of his arms was all that was sustaining her. He gave her a deep kiss before he reluctantly relinquished her lips. They were both out of breath when he let go of her.

"We have so much to talk about, but until Seth's trial

is over, I can't be alone like this with you again. In fact, to make sure this doesn't happen, I'm turning your case over to Chief Wayland in the morning while I work behind the scenes. He'll assign his best detective to keep you briefed. You'll be hearing from him by tomorrow."

He started walking toward the door. Panicked, she followed him. "I don't want anyone else to handle this, Holden. Why don't you and I agree that because we've both lost a spouse, it was inevitable that something like this was bound to happen in time?"

He shook his head. "I broke my own cardinal rule tonight. When Seth is sentenced, then we'll be able to be together the way I want."

She couldn't let him go. "Don't forget you had help, Holden Granger. For your information, I'm *not* sorry!"

He looked tormented. "Surely you realize I only want you. What will I tell Chase after we've made plans to vacation together? Please don't let what happened between us today change anything."

"It already has."

"Promise me you won't pull away, if only for Chase's sake."

She heard his sharp intake of breath. "You don't know what you're asking," he said before disappearing down the stairs. Jessica knew he was due back at headquarters.

She took a few minutes to compose herself and was about to leave the apartment when her mother walked in. "I just saw Holden drive away."

"Yes. He's gone back to headquarters."

"Did he tell you about the arraignment?"

"Oh, Mom." She broke down and told her everything.

"Honey? I'm sorry the judge ruled the way he did, but Holden said he'd protect you and Chase. He also told you he'll put Seth under constant surveillance when he leaves the jail tomorrow."

"I know."

"So what's wrong?" Her mother studied her for a minute. "I thought you'd be floating on air today, even if Seth did get bail. Instead, I haven't seen you this down in two years."

"That's because Holden says we shouldn't be together until the trial is over. For Chase's sake, I begged him not to stay away. But I have another dilemma, too."

"What is it?"

"I wasn't honest with Holden from the beginning. I'm in love with him, but I can't be!"

"Is that because you feel like you're betraying Trent's memory?"

"No, Mom—nothing like that."

Her mother looked bewildered. "Then help me understand."

Jessica hid her face in her hands. "It's because I have no right to love him."

"Has he told you he loves you?"

"Just before you came, he kissed me and said he was in love with me."

"And that makes you unhappy?"

"You've seen the way he is with Chase." Tears stung her eyes. "He's going to be the most fantastic father one day."

"Ah… Now I know where you're going with this. He has no idea you can't have more children."

"No, and I should have told him in the beginning.

After he left the house last night, I cried for hours. I know I have to tell him, but I'm scared."

Her mother walked over and hugged her for a long time. "When you leave, go get Chase and bring him back here. I've invited Ray for dinner. We can all eat together and Ray and I will watch Chase while you go to Holden's office to have a talk with him.

"Honey, don't presume to know what he's thinking or feeling. Let me ask you something. If your situations were reversed, don't you think you would have found it strange if, in the beginning, the sheriff, a stranger to you, had told you upfront he was a widower who couldn't give a woman a child?"

"Of course it would have been strange."

"Then don't blame yourself for not saying anything to him about your condition. This is all a moot point since you've both admitted you're in love. You have to get beyond this."

Sometimes Jessica's mother was so sensible, it was scary. "Thanks for listening to me, Mom, and offering to watch Chase. I love you."

Holden wheeled away from the salon and drove to headquarters. It was amazing he'd been able to stop kissing Jessica when he did. For a few minutes he'd forgotten where he was or why. All he knew was his desire for the beautiful woman who'd put her trust in him from the beginning.

Her response to him had broken through every defense. His personal life had been a desert for so long, the wonder of kissing her had knocked him off-balance.

But he had to keep his head on straight until the trial when Seth was incarcerated. Once this case was closed, then he could be with her the way he'd imagined in his dreams.

On his way back, he met O.J. at the Blue Bird for one of their usual quick meals. He owed the fire chief a bunch of lunches. Holden found his friend already seated and patted him on the shoulder before ordering. "You're one of the people I have to thank for this red-letter day."

"Yeah?" O.J. smiled at him.

"The guy I've been after was just arraigned in court. His trial is coming up soon, but I can tell you the facts now. Two years ago Trent Fleming, a top mechanic at Mid-Valley dealership died in a car crash testing his wife's car after replacing the ball joints. It turns out someone had tampered with that car. His name is Seth Lunt. He was a service writer at Mid-Valley. This guy is a true psychopath."

While they ate, Holden regaled his friend with some of the details. "Thanks to you for sending Porter on that search, I was able to get hold of the surveillance tapes that proved Seth removed one of the new Moog ball joints and put in a faulty one during the night. It caused the wheel to come off and the car overturned in the rain. Forensics retrieved Seth's thumbprint off it. I'm indebted to you for your help."

O.J.'s face broke out in a smile. "I couldn't be happier for you. So how come this particular case has been so important to you?"

"That's still classified."

"I knew it." His friend roared with laughter. "How long do I have to wait?"

"Hopefully not long. Now I have to go." Holden put some bills on the table to pay for both their lunches.

"Thanks for taking the time to meet with me. If you ever need a favor from me, I'm your man."

Holden went back to the office, taking his leftovers with him. From now until the weekend, he was on duty so Walt could have some well-deserved time off.

Once behind his desk he sent a text to Porter thanking him for his help checking out the dealership on a fire inspection. He asked him to call when he had a chance. Then Holden started on the paperwork piled up on his desk.

He was running on autopilot. Jessica loved him. Kissing her and being kissed back had unlocked his passion. He was madly in love, but he had to be careful when they were together. She was right. He couldn't disappoint her son by staying away. The best way to handle things was to make sure Chase was always with them. That would help Holden keep his desire in check.

While he sat there trying to convince himself that plan would work, he received a text from Jessica that she'd arrived at headquarters. He couldn't believe it and told Deputy Sykes to let her in.

With a pounding heart, he got up and walked to the doorway of his office. In a minute, he heard footsteps coming around the corner and down the empty hall. She looked breathtaking in tan pants and a ruffled peach blouse. Her lipstick on that mouth he'd kissed over and over earlier today matched her blouse.

As she drew closer he said, "You look like you just walked off the page of a fashion magazine."

"Thank you." But she averted those green eyes he couldn't get enough of. "I'm sorry to come here like this uninvited, but I have to talk to you. Do you mind?"

"If you have to ask me that, then you didn't hear one word I told you this afternoon."

"Yes, I did. I could have texted you, but you don't get the context if there's no voice or emotion accompanying it."

He noticed she was nervous and talking too fast. "Since being with you this afternoon, I haven't accomplished anything. This is like a gift. Come in and sit down."

"Thank you." Jessica sat on one of the chairs in front of his desk.

He lounged against a corner of it with his arms folded.

"I'm thankful to see you have some quiet times between all the emergencies that put your life in danger, Holden. You work way too hard."

"I like it."

She clasped her hands tightly before looking at him. "Thank heaven for you."

She was once again acting like the warm, wonderful woman he wanted in his life forever. Holden couldn't figure out what was going on with her. "Tell me what's wrong. I didn't expect to see you tonight."

"I'm sorry, Holden. I've been trying to build up the courage to talk to you since you left my mother's apartment."

Courage? The word gutted him. He couldn't begin to imagine the reasons why the temperature had fallen from a hundred to zero. What had happened to cause a shift in the earth's rotation? 'Cause that was what it felt like.

"Is it because you're still too in love with the memory of your husband to consider a relationship with me? Deep down I've feared your guilt would eventually overwhelm you. That's because I've been through a similar experience.

"When I came to Whitebark, I tried dating a couple of women, but it didn't work. I couldn't get Cynthia out of my mind and had to end things before they could begin. But the situation with you has been completely different for me.

"I found myself developing feelings for you and didn't experience the guilt. That's when I knew I had to let go of the past. But because you're not where I am emotionally, you don't have to say another word. I get it."

She seemed to pale before she got to her feet. "You're wrong about everything you've just said where I'm concerned. I came here for one reason only—to apologize for not telling you the truth about me when we first met. It was unfair to you."

Holden moved away from the desk. What was she saying now? "*What* truth about you?" His blood curdled in dread as certain implications of her remark took hold of him.

"Once we started being together, I was so wrong to keep this from you."

He couldn't handle this another second. "Tell me!"

"I—I can't have more children—" Her voice faltered.

The answer was so unexpected, and so far from his fear that she might be dying of a disease that he couldn't take it in.

"After Chase was born, we'd hoped to give him a sister or brother, but we couldn't get pregnant. I went through months of testing. Finally, the specialist diagnosed me with a condition called early menopause. Every possible avenue for having my own baby with the man I love was closed to me. At first I didn't want to believe it and suffered for a long time.

"After Trent was killed, I decided the fates were against me. I had to live for Chase. He's my life, but outside of him I've had to fight to get back my love for everything that was once important to me.

"Since meeting you, I've returned to the world I used to love. That's what you've done for me. But I was wrong not to let you know about my condition the second you told me about losing your wife to cancer. Forgive me. If anyone was meant to have children one day, it's you."

"Jessica..."

"You'd be wasting your time to spend one more minute with me. That's what I came to tell you. You already know I love you, Holden, and I'll never forget you as long as I live."

Holden was so stunned by her revelation, and so relieved to know she wasn't dying, he wasn't prepared when she started to leave his office. He raced after her and pulled her back against him until she relaxed in his arms.

"Listen to me." He buried his face in her hair. "There's nothing to forgive. Being unable to have more children isn't something you tell someone as soon as you meet. I thought you were about to tell me you had a life-threatening disease and didn't have long to live. Don't you realize I can handle anything as long as I know nothing's wrong with you?"

Jessica whirled around in his arms and lifted her wet, beautiful face to his.

"I'm so sorry. After what you've lived through with Cynthia, I should have come right out with it when I walked in this office the first time. But it doesn't take away from the fact that there *is* something wrong with me. Horribly wrong. For you to go on seeing me keeps you from meeting other women who want and are able to have babies with you. *Your* babies."

"I don't want another woman."

"But I can't do the one thing that brings ultimate joy. When I told Trent we were expecting, he was so happy it turned him into a whole different man. I saw it. If you decide you want to marry again, you need to find a woman who can do that for you."

"Please don't back away from me, Jessica."

To his chagrin, she was beyond hearing him for the moment. "You should be able to have your own little boy who adores his daddy. I'm not going to see you anymore."

He took a sharp breath. "You can't do that."

"I have to."

"How will you explain this to Chase?"

"I'll figure it out." She made a turn to leave.

"Wait—"

"I can't. Mom's watching Chase and it's getting late. I shouldn't even be here now while you're on call." Her moist eyes lifted to his one last time. "God bless you, Sheriff Granger. You're the absolute best of the best and will always be the hero of the entire Fleming family."

Holden knew this wasn't the time to stop her. Jessica was so convinced she was doing the right thing, she was in no mood to listen to him right now. He admired that strong will of hers, but she'd underestimated the strength of his love.

At ten thirty he called it a night and left headquarters for home.

Knowing he wouldn't be able to sleep yet, he shrugged on a robe and went out on his back porch. The stars filled the heavens and the familiar scent of sage permeated the warm air. A night like this stirred all his senses. His desire for Jessica was eating him alive.

I can't have more children.

He'd heard the agony in her voice as she told him that fact. Only now did he realize he *was* devastated, for himself and for her. Since meeting her he'd imagined them being together and raising a family. It hurt him to know that if they married, they would never have a baby together. After getting to know Jessica and Chase, he realized that was what he truly wanted.

But as sad as that made him, it was nothing compared to the thought of losing her. He'd told her he didn't want another woman. That declaration had poured unedited from the depths of his soul. He couldn't take it back because it was the truth.

He went to bed and for the rest of the night he laid out the plan in his mind to win her back. When Thursday morning dawned, he showered and shaved. After putting on a clean uniform, he left a message for his house cleaning service that came once a month.

On his way to the office, he grabbed a bite of breakfast. Following that, he went to the office to draw up a new schedule for the deputies patrolling the city and outskirts. After letting Jenny in dispatch know he was on call even though he was leaving the office for a while, he put on his sheriff's hat and drove to Weaver's Fine Jewelry.

Matt Weaver, the owner, smiled when he saw him. Holden had covered a break-in at the store last year. "Sheriff? I hope this isn't official business this time."

"Only of a personal nature," he said.

"Ah, I see."

"I want to buy a one-carat solitaire diamond ring set in white gold. Nothing gaudy." That wasn't Jessica's style. "What have you got to show me?"

The jeweler did a double take. "They're right down here."

Holden walked to the next counter. Matt put a tray of rings on top of the glass. "Do you see anything you like? The princess cut is very popular. So is the marquis."

They all looked beautiful, but the round cut stood out to Holden. "May I see this one?"

The owner handed it to him for closer inspection. "You've picked the most traditional cut. You also have a fine eye. This one at $6,000 is an E-grade exceptional white diamond with an SI2 flawless clarity rating. What is the ring size you need?"

"I'm not sure. She's five feet six and probably weighs 120 pounds."

Matt nodded. "If you want this diamond, I'll mount it on the right sized band."

"How long will it take you?"

"Two minutes."

"Terrific. I'll wait."

While the jeweler changed the diamond to a different sized band, Holden pulled out his wallet to get his credit card. Matt came back with the ring in a little black velvet box.

"That's perfect." Holden handed him the card.

"If the size isn't right, have her come in. Do you want me to gift wrap it?"

"No, thanks. I plan to give it to her just like this." As soon as possible. There was no time to lose.

"Congratulations, Sheriff."

"Thank you. Do me a favor and don't tell anyone."

"My lips are sealed. Whoever she is, she's a very lucky woman."

"She's the love of my life."

Holden put the box in his chest pocket and walked outside to his truck. He headed to work until noon, then asked Deputy Sykes to cover for him for an hour and drove to Style Clips. There was a parking space near the entrance.

Her mother was busy when he walked in. She smiled at him. "Jessica is upstairs. You can go up. She's alone right now."

"Thanks."

He walked through the salon and took the stairs two at a time to the apartment above.

Taking a deep breath, he knocked on the door.

"Mom?"

A second later, she opened it. Her face glistened with tears. *"Holden—"* She backed away from him. "What are you doing here?"

"Maybe this will explain."

To her shock, he threw his cap on the nearest chair and got down on one knee. Looking up at her, he said, "Jessica Fleming? Will you marry me?" He pulled the little black velvet box out of his uniform pocket and opened it for her.

She actually cried out when she saw the exquisite diamond solitaire ring winking up at her. He put the box in her hand.

"I don't care if it's impossible to get you pregnant. I'm in love with you and want to live the rest of my life with you and no one else. I won't lie to you. It hurt to hear about your condition, but having a baby isn't the reason I want you to be my wife. With you I've found my other half. You make me happy I'm alive.

"If you push me away, you're condemning me to a life of pain and emptiness I don't want to think about. Do you hear what I'm saying?" He got to his feet. "I already love Chase. Given time maybe he'll let me be a father to him."

"Holden—"

"Don't say anything right now. I can see in your eyes you still don't believe me. But I had all night to consider what it means not to have children with you and it doesn't matter. I love *you*. That's it for me. Now I'm late for work and might not have a job if I don't accomplish something today. Text me your answer."

Chapter 11

Before Jessica could stop him, he grabbed his hat and flew out the door. Once again, Holden had misread her.

She stood there with the ring box in her hand, so overjoyed by what had just happened, she felt like she was in a trance.

Her mom texted her. She heard the little ding and knew she needed to go downstairs to take care of her next client. But as much as she was dying to put the ring on, she wanted Holden to do it.

After slipping the box in her jeans pocket, she went downstairs and tried to pretend in front of her mother that Holden's visit had to do with the case. For the rest of the day she kept quiet. Later, after she'd picked up Chase, she'd call her mother and they'd talk.

Jessica couldn't remember her feet touching the ground once she'd gone home to exercise Bucky. Chase helped her fix enchiladas for dinner. "When's Holden going to come over again?"

"I have an idea how we can find out, honey. After I shower and get dressed, let's drive over to headquarters and see Holden. We'll take him some dinner. If he's there, I'm sure he won't mind if we stop by and make plans with him. You can ask him all the questions you want."

A half hour later, they drove into town. As usual, Chase wore his hat. She parked in front of headquarters and texted Holden.

I'm out in front. Will you ask Deputy Sykes to let me in?

Her pulse raced when he answered almost immediately that his deputy would look for her.

After they got out of her car, Chase carried the dinner plate covered in foil to the main entrance. The deputy smiled at them. "Come on in. The sheriff is waiting for you. Smells like you've brought him something good to eat."

"Yup," Chase said. "We made dinner for him."

"How lucky can a man get. Hey—where did you get that hat?"

"Holden gave it to me."

"Well, how about that?"

"We're friends. Come on, Mom."

She smiled at the deputy before hurrying after her son. He knew exactly where to go. Holden met them when they were halfway down the hall. Surprise lit his eyes to see she'd brought Chase with her.

Holden approached Chase. "What's going on?"

"We brought your dinner. I helped make it."

"How did you know I was starving? I can't wait to eat it. Thanks!"

The three of them walked the rest of the way to his office. He sat behind his desk and took the foil off the plate. "Oh, boy. Enchiladas. My favorite! You even brought me a fork. Can I dig in?"

Chase stood next to him. "Yup. Mom said you'd be hungry."

Holden's all-encompassing gaze focused on her. "She was right. Guess what? I loaded up with groceries earlier this week. Tomorrow I'll drive you over to my house and we'll pack a lot of sandwiches and treats and we'll go on a hike."

Chase let out a sound of excitement. "Is it okay if I bring my backpack?"

"That'll be perfect. Then we'll be able to carry everything."

The phone rang on the desk, interrupting them. Holden picked up and talked police business. Probably a deputy. Jessica waited until he hung up.

"You're busy, and we only came to bring you dinner. Since we're going on a hike tomorrow, we need to get home to bed. But before we go, I wanted to show Chase what you gave me today. I couldn't believe you had to leave the salon before you could put it on my finger."

Her heart pounded heavily as she pulled the ring box out of her purse and handed it to Holden. When he opened it, the emotion coming from his eyes took her breath away.

Chase looked at her. "Hey—that's a ring!"

"A very special one, Chase," Holden said in a husky voice. "It means I love your mother."

"She loves you, too."

Jessica could tell Holden was totally taken aback. "That makes me very happy. Did your mother tell you?"

"Nope. But I've been praying."

"Chase, honey—"

Holden got up and walked around the desk. Looking down at her, he reached for her left hand and slid the ring on her ring finger.

Chase moved close to him. "Are you going to get married?"

Her heart skipped a beat waiting for Holden's answer.

"How would you feel about that, Chase?"

"Since my real dad died, I *want* you to be my dad."

The moment was one Jessica would remember all her life as she watched Holden sweep him up in his arms. Those silver eyes had teared up. "Guess what? The first time I met you, I wished I had a boy just like you. That's why I gave you my own hat. I love you more than anything, Chase."

"I love you, too!" He kissed Holden's hard jaw. "Wait till I tell Joey the sheriff is going to be my new dad!"

Of course the phone would ring at that tender moment. Holden reached for it. After a moment, he lowered Chase to the floor. "I've got to go. Deputy Sykes will see you out."

"Don't worry about us." This would be their life from now on. She'd better get used to it. Holden pressed a kiss to her mouth before dashing out of the room and down the hall.

Chase looked up at her, but he still wore a smile. "I bet he has to catch a bad guy."

"While he does that, we need to leave." Jessica rolled

up the empty paper plate with the foil and put it in the wastebasket. The movement caused the sparkle from the diamond to catch the light and dazzle her eyes. "On our way home, let's stop at Nana's for a minute. She won't be in bed yet. I want to show her my engagement ring."

When they reached the salon, Chase told her mom the great news and Jessica's mother let out a cry of joy.

There was so much to tell her mom, but that could wait. All Jessica said was, "When Holden told me he would live with pain and emptiness for the rest of his life without me, he was describing how I felt to turn him down. I couldn't do it."

The three of them hugged before Jessica and Chase left to go home. Jessica figured she wouldn't hear from Holden until morning. Chase got down on his knees to say his prayers. It took longer than usual. Then he came to the end. "Thank you for giving me Holden for a new dad. I never wanted anyone else, 'specially not Seth. Amen."

That name froze Jessica to the bone. She helped her son get under the covers. "Chase? Why did you mention Seth?"

"He told me he liked you, but I had to keep it a secret."

Sickness rose in her throat. "When did he tell you that?"

"When he gave me the truck."

"Why didn't you tell me?"

"He got mad when you weren't there. It scared me. I'm glad we don't have to go to Dad's work anymore."

"Oh, honey—" She held her boy close for a minute.

His behavior was no longer a mystery. "You don't have to be afraid anymore."

"I know. Holden will keep us safe."

"He'll always do everything in his power to protect us."

Years from now she and Holden would tell him why Trent really had that accident.

Her son threw his arms around her neck. "I love Holden so much."

"So do I. Now it's time to sleep. Just think. Tomorrow we'll all be together for the whole day."

Since Holden had to leave, he took advantage of the time to phone his parents and tell them the news. He'd already told them last week that he was bringing a woman and her five-year-old son to Cody with him soon. They hadn't asked a lot of questions, but had to know it was important.

After the grief he'd gone through losing Cynthia, they had to have wondered how long it would take before he met someone else. But when he got them on the phone and asked them to turn on the speaker, they couldn't hide their shock when he told them he and Jessica Fleming would be planning their wedding soon.

"How long have you known her?"

"A month, maybe a little more."

"So fast?" his mother cried.

"When you meet Jessica and her son, you'll understand why I fell so hard."

"Holden," his father chimed in, "this doesn't sound like you."

"I agree. She came into my office just over a month ago, fearing that her husband—who was killed in a car crash two years ago—had been murdered. By the time she left, I knew I'd lost my heart." His voice throbbed.

"Murdered?"

"Yes." For the next few minutes he explained what he'd discovered and how it had led to the ultimate arrest of Seth Lunt. "Throughout the investigation we were either together or in touch constantly. After the killer was arraigned, I bought a ring and asked her to marry me."

Silence came from their end.

"Have you met her parents?"

"Only her mother, who is wonderful."

"Where's her father?"

"He was killed when she was in her early teens, Mom."

"How tragic."

"But she had great family support. When we drive to Cody, we'll talk over our plans with you and set a date for the wedding. It will have to be after the trial on the seventh. I'm thinking the tenth or so of July. Be thinking about some dates that work for you. We'll want it to be soon."

"Good heavens."

It was a lot for them to absorb at once.

"I'll be trailing Blackie and Jessica's horse, Bucky. Her husband once competed in the pro rodeo as a bull rider. Maybe we'll be bringing a pony for Chase."

"Holden?" his father broke in. "Naturally, we're thrilled you've found another woman to fill your heart. The whole family will be thrilled."

"Thank you. You couldn't ask for a more wonderful boy. I love him like a son already. You will, too."

"We can't wait to meet both of them." His mother was all choked up.

"I took pictures of them on my phone while we were on a hike a while back. I'm texting them to you now. Take a look." He waited to give them time to look at the photos.

"She's beautiful!" his mother blurted. "And that boy is adorable! He's wearing your sheriff's hat!"

Holden smiled. "I gave him mine and had to order another one."

"I like that photo of the three of you." This from his dad. "You all look great together."

"We *are* great together."

"I've never heard you so happy."

"I am, Mom. Now I've got to go, but I'll be in touch."

Before he left the office, he phoned Jessica. She answered on the second ring. "I'm so glad you called."

"Are you home?"

"Yes, and Chase is in bed."

"Does your mother know we're engaged?"

"Yes, and she's overjoyed! I knew I wouldn't sleep until we talked."

"I've got the same problem. I just broke the news to my folks and sent them pictures. They can't wait to meet you. Just to prepare them, I said we hope to get married around the tenth."

"How did they react?"

"Silence at first. Then they got the nutshell version of our courtship. But the pictures I sent to them over the phone did the trick. They can't wait to meet you and Chase. What's important is that they're happy for us."

"I feel like I'm in a dream. I wish you were here

now. Holden—I love you so much you'll never know. I need you to kiss me and never stop."

"When the trial is over, you're going to get your wish for the rest of our lives, my love. I adore you. Now I should let you go. See you tomorrow."

After leaving his office, he headed home. Holden had been asleep only three hours when his phone rang. Feeling for the phone on the bedside table, he answered. "Sheriff Granger."

"Sheriff? It's Deputy Green. Seth Lunt just escaped house arrest."

He felt like he'd been slugged and jumped out of bed. "How did that happen when we have the house covered?" Quickly, he threw on his uniform, having had a hunch this moment would come.

"Dispatch took a call from his mother moments ago when she saw Seth shoot her husband. The officers heard a shot and saw he had a gun as he dragged her out to the Lexus with him, using her as a shield before he took off. We've got other units trailing him now.

"Chief Wayland has sent more units to the Lunt house and asked me to work with you. He's put out an all-points bulletin to shoot Lunt on sight, but urges caution because Mrs. Lunt is his captive. Roadblocks have been ordered."

"Where are you?"

"At Mrs. Fleming's ranch house. So far Seth hasn't shown up here yet."

"Thank God. I'll head for the beauty salon."

"Deputy Romero has it covered. So far no sign of him there, either. I think he may be coming for you, Sheriff."

His eyes closed tightly. "I think you could be right,

Rick." Holden wouldn't forget that malevolent look in Seth's eyes during the arraignment. "If he comes on my property, he'll probably head for the barn."

"I'm headed your way now with more deputies following. Just a minute. Sheriff? I just got two messages. Mr. Lunt died on the way to the hospital and Seth is nowhere inside or outside Style Clips."

"Understood. We'll stay in touch."

Holden reached for his night-vision goggles and small bag of tools, then ran out the back door to the barn under a dark cloudy sky. He got into a tuck position to scan his property through the glasses. Since he'd received no message that Seth had been spotted anywhere else, he would wait here for him as long as it took. The roadblocks would stop him if he planned to cross state lines.

An hour went by. Holden was convinced Lunt was hidden along some private road near the house, planning out his next move. Time passed. When it got to be 4:00 a.m., Holden crept back toward his house wearing his goggles. He still didn't see movement.

He moved to the side of the garage, then stole around to the front of it. Something told him Seth could have gotten inside the house by breaking a back window. He could be waiting for him in the garage.

It didn't take Holden long to remove the four bolts that held up the mechanism to lift the door. When he undid the coupling, he would be able to open the garage door manually.

If Seth was inside, he would hear the noise and hopefully give himself away.

With his weapon in one hand, Holden lifted the door. His car and truck filled the space. Holden crouched down to see if Seth was hiding under either of them. That was when he saw broken glass on the cement beneath the front passenger door of the car.

Seth had broken into it. Most likely, he was lying on the floor of the back seat holding the gun that had killed his father. Who knew what he'd done to his mother, or where he'd abandoned her.

Holden continued to move around. Ever so carefully, he lifted his hand through the gaping hole and pressed on the horn, alerting the deputies outside. The sound could have wakened the dead. That brought Seth's head up over the seat. He was brandishing his gun, but Holden had him covered.

"Don't move, Lunt. You're surrounded and don't have a chance of getting away."

"You bastard." He shot at Holden. The bullet went zinging past his ear, but he felt a jolt of pain in his hand.

"Put down your weapon," one of the SWAT team guys called out.

Seth answered with two more shots. Holden crawled along the side of the car to get behind it where he would have more of an advantage. But Seth had opened the rear door. The next thing Holden knew, his own gun dropped to the ground.

At that point, the officers swarmed in to take Seth, but Holden heard one more shot. Another voice said, "The suspect turned the gun on himself."

Holden got up and moved closer. Any death was a terrible thing, but to see the blood on Seth Lunt's long hair and know he'd taken himself out filled Holden with relief of an entirely different kind. The sick man never got the chance to hurt Jessica and would never be a menace to anyone again.

He reeled, dizzy with relief. Chief Wayland was there to steady him with a hand on his shoulder. "Congratulations on nailing him. Come on. The paramedics are waiting. Let's get you to the hospital so they can fix that hand."

"But my goggles are around the side of the garage and my gun is in here somewhere. I need to call Jessica. I'm supposed to be taking her and Chase on a hike in a little while."

"No, you don't." The chief took the phone from him. "You need fixing up or you're going to pass out before you talk to her."

"I've never needed an ambulance and I don't need one now."

The chief ignored him and the paramedics took over until they drove him to the hospital and wheeled him into the emergency room with an IV in his arm. Wayland walked in a moment later. "We're taking care of things. It's time to take care of you."

"But I have to call Jessica."

"It's five thirty in the morning. You can call Mrs. Fleming after the doctor has taken care of you."

Holden was forced to lie back while the doctor examined him. The chief waited in the ER while the doctor sent him to X-ray. When he was brought back, the two of them talked. Wayland told him the sad news that Seth had killed his mother, too. They'd found her body in the Lexus on the road leading into the Simpson's Ranch.

"I have good news, Sheriff," the surgeon said after coming in the cubicle. "The bullet grazed the baby finger on your left hand. It fractured the bone and did a little soft tissue damage. But there are no other complications and won't be if you take your antibiotics. I'll put a splint on your pinky. The bone will knit back and you'll be good as new in about six weeks."

"How soon can I go home?"

"As soon I put on the splint."

In another half hour, Holden's vital signs checked out and he was released. The sun had just come up over the horizon when the chief drove him back to his ranch and helped him inside the house. "I'm good from here. Thanks, man. I'm indebted to you."

"I'm glad to hear it, but take it easy, Holden. You're going to need help."

He grinned. "I know, and I'll get it if you'll leave so I can call her."

Holden heard the chief's laughter all the way to his van before he went inside and headed for the bedroom. After lying down on the bed, he pulled the phone from his pocket. It was good the bullet had hit his left hand. Being right-handed, he could still manage everything he needed to do and made the phone call that was going to set Jessica free.

"Holden?" she answered on the second ring. "How did you know I woke up thinking about you and am dying for you to come over?"

He smiled. "That's nice to hear. But I've been forced to change our plans for today."

"What's wrong?"

"Do you want the good news or the bad news first?"

"What do you think I should hear first?" she asked quietly.

"Our worries about Seth are over forever. He killed himself early this morning."

"*What?* Holden!"

"It's a sad story. He killed his parents, too. I'll tell you all about it as soon as you and Chase drive over to my house."

After a silence, she said, "What's wrong with you? What did he do to you?" He heard the tremor in her voice.

"He took a shot at me inside my garage and hit my pinky. It has a little splint on it, but will be all better in about six weeks. I have to stay down today according to the doctor and would love some TLC from you and Chase."

"Oh, darling—we'll be over as soon as I wake up Chase."

"Hurry. I left the door open."

She clicked off so fast, he laughed. Within a minute, his phone rang. He saw the caller ID and picked up, euphoric that he and Jessica could get married without delay.

"Porter, my man."

"The guys and I just heard the news. We're back from a fire at the Rockford ranch and pulled up in front of your house. We're coming in."

"The door's open."

In a minute, his friends Cole, Porter and Wyatt came into the bedroom in their firefighter hurry-ups smelling of smoke.

"Don't worry." Wyatt grinned. "We won't sit down. Captain Durrant is waiting out in the truck for us."

"How did you guys find out?"

"Are you kidding? Chief Wayland got on the horn to Chief Powell and by now everybody knows including the governor. The chief says you'll be getting a citation. It'll be on the news. Both departments are buzzing about how you caught the guy who killed Trent Fleming. You're a hero, dude. Way to go! We heard he shot your little finger before he took himself out."

Holden lifted his hand to show them the splint.

Cole shook his head. "Between us, we think Judge Garson was an idiot to release a killer on bail. We heard Chief Wayland is going to look into it."

"I was surprised Judge Jenkins didn't preside, but it doesn't matter now."

"We're just thankful you're alive, you know."

"So am I," Holden murmured. "Did I tell you I'm getting married?"

"Congratulations!"

Porter smiled. "We figured you had to be hung up on Jessica Fleming because you've been missing from our poker parties for the last month. She's a knockout."

"She *is* that, and a lot more. I fell for her the first moment she came to the office to tell me she didn't think her husband died because of an accident two years ago. We got engaged last night. You know she has a five-year-old son, Chase? The kid is incredible. Jessica's mother owns the Style Clips salon. Jessica is a beautician like her mom."

"Tamsin knows her," Cole said. "She goes there to get her hair done and thinks the world of her."

Porter whistled. "It looks like I'm the last loser left in Whitebark with no love life."

"I was where you are before that blizzard dropped Alex at my tent door," Wyatt exclaimed. "Don't worry. Your turn is coming."

Holden nodded. "It can happen that fast when the right one comes along."

"We're happy for you, Holden."

"Thanks, Wyatt. I'll call you guys as soon as we know our plans. I want the three of you at the wedding and our reception."

"Do you have any idea when it'll be?"

"As soon as Jessica gets over here so we can make it happen."

Porter chuckled. "Put all of us on your list, and save us a night to throw you a bachelor party."

"I promise."

"Chief Wayland said you have to stay down for a day or two. Some of us will be over later. Anything we can bring you?"

"Just yourselves. You're the best medicine I know of."

Five minutes after the guys left his bedroom he heard an excited young voice.

"Holden?"

The loves of his life had just arrived.

Chapter 12

Jessica had been prepared that Holden had suffered a wound to his pinky finger. But she'd never seen him incapacitated in any way. The sight of him lying on his bed in his uniform with a splint on his left hand shook her. It could have been so much worse.

She let Chase run to him first. After hugs, Holden had her son laughing within seconds.

"You know what? I'm thirsty for a cold drink. Could you run out to the kitchen and find me a soda? Get yourself one, too, if you want. I bought a lot of stuff for our hike, so pick whatever sounds good. We'll go on a hike another time when I'm better."

"Yup. Mom says you have to stay in bed for a while. I'll be right back. Do you want a drink, too, Mom?"

"Not right now, thank you, honey."

The second he left the room, she rushed over to the

bed and threw her arms around Holden's neck. "Thank God you're alive and it's over!"

Once she felt his mouth cover hers, desire swept through her. One hungry kiss followed another, each one growing longer and deeper until he set her on fire. Too much pleasure caused her to moan. The knowledge that there were no more shadows had made her joy complete. Nothing would ever separate them again.

Just one month ago, while she'd been cleaning the garage, she couldn't have imagined being in love like this again. This sensational man was going to be her husband. She felt as if she were caught up in a whirlwind. "I love you, Holden. I love you," she whispered into his neck.

His lips roved over her face, kissing every feature. "If we go on like this another second, I'm going to eat you alive. I'd rather wait until we say our vows at the altar before I make love to you, so we need to set a date as soon as we can."

Chase came back in the bedroom with their drinks and she helped Holden sit up against the headboard.

"Here's a cola for you and a root beer for me. I brought some potato chips, too." Their favorite kind.

Holden patted the other side of the bed so Chase could sit. The two of them drank their sodas and munched on the chips. Jessica took Holden's empty can and put it on the bedside table. Then he grasped her hand with his right hand and clung to it.

"How soon are you two going to get married?"

"I'm glad you asked, Chase. We'll plan it right now."

"Hooray! Are we going to live in your house or mine?"

Both she and Holden chuckled. Jessica was giddy with happiness. "What would you like?" he asked.

"Will you live at our house? You could bring Blackie over and put him in the barn with Bucky."

"That sounds like a perfect idea. Maybe we could buy Sparky and he could live with us, too."

"Yeah. Are you going to have a big wedding?"

"The biggest, pardner."

"How would you like to wear a tuxedo?" Jessica asked her son.

"What's a 'tuck-see-do'?"

Holden roared with laughter. "I call it a penguin suit. They're black-and-white. I'll wear one, too. And after we get married at your church, we'll have a reception at the Whitebark Hotel and invite Joey and your other friends to come."

"Can I tell Joey right now?"

Jessica was overjoyed. *Yes, yes, yes.* "I'll phone Wilma's number right now."

"Goody!"

"Take my phone in the living room to talk to him."

Chase came around the bed and took it from her before running out of the bedroom with the bag of chips.

The second they were alone, Holden pulled her down on top of him. *"Jessica—"* He crushed her against his body and kissed her possessively. The world spun away now that they were able to shower their love on each other. "You have no idea how much I love you." In the next breath they were devouring each other.

"I wish we were on our honeymoon right now," she murmured. "Ugh… I'm afraid I sound like Chase."

"We're going to need one. I love it. I love you. On Monday we'll go get our marriage license. We don't need a blood test and there's no waiting period. As soon as we pick a date, we'll arrange it with your pastor."

By the time Chase come running back in, they were entwined and had to break apart.

"Joey can't wait!"

"Neither can I," Holden whispered against Jessica's lips and he kissed her one more time before setting her free. Jessica was so deliriously happy she couldn't believe she wasn't dreaming.

"You know what this means, Chase? Tomorrow I'll be well enough for the three of us to leave for Cody for a few days. I want you to meet my family. They know we're getting married and are dying to meet you before the wedding. You're going to love Chrissy and Rob."

"Can we go, Mom?" Chase's eyes were dancing.

Her heart was so full, she could hardly talk. "I'll call Nana and tell her our plans."

Holden's eyes held hers. "On our way back from Cody, we'll pick up the marriage license."

After a five-hundred-mile drive that had started out Sunday morning, the three of them arrived in Cody.

"Here we are, Chase."

His brown eyes rounded. "Your family lives in a *huge* ranch house!"

That produced a deep chuckle from Holden.

Jessica's son was right. The sprawling two-story log-style ranch house looked to be right off the cover of *Old West* magazine.

Ponderosa and cottonwood trees shaded most of it with well-tended lush green grass and flowers in front. Good heavens! She'd had no idea.

There were so many things she still didn't know

about Holden. So little time and the urgency of circumstances had prevented them from learning even some of the most elemental things about each other's lives.

The second they'd driven underneath the arch of antlers holding up the sign Circle G Ranch, Jessica had understood that he came from a well-to-do ranching family that likely went back many generations. The mention of his own property that adjoined his father's should have given her a clue.

"Is this yours?"

"It belongs to the Granger family." She marveled at Holden's patience at answering Chase's questions.

"How big is it?"

"Eight thousand acres."

"That's a lot, huh, Mom?"

"I'll say." Jessica was still trying to take it all in.

"It has to be big, Chase. We're a cattle ranch."

"Do you have a lot of cows?"

"About a thousand mother cows and five hundred babies."

Chase looked at Jessica. "Mom? I'm not afraid of cows."

All three of them laughed. Jessica squeezed Holden's arm. "Of course not. They're gentle."

Holden smiled at Jessica. He knew how much of a surprise this was to her and Chase. "I'll drive us around to the corral so Blackie and Bucky can go for a run. Then we'll go in the house and you can meet my family."

They drove around to some outbuildings and a large barn. Beyond it were several corrals and livestock facilities. Holden was a remarkable man to have left all this and moved to Whitebark. If he hadn't come, Jessica would never have met him. That was something she couldn't contemplate. Not now.

After he parked the truck next to the barn, he got out. Jessica opened her door and jumped down to help him with the horses.

The horses seemed to have handled the trip well. But Bucky acted happy to see her when Holden opened the doors and she walked around to him.

"How are you doing, fella?" He nickered several times. She patted his neck and backed him out of the trailer to where Chase was waiting. "We've brought you to a new place, Bucky. Come on. We'll walk you around so you get used to it."

Holden did the same thing with Blackie, his black gelding who was almost as gorgeous as his master. But the minute Holden entered the corral, he let Blackie go and his horse took off, acting very much at home.

Bucky was a little more timid. Jessica removed the lead rope. "Let's take a walk." Chase watched from the top of the corral fencing. She started ahead of the horse. Pretty soon, he followed her. She headed for Blackie to see what Bucky would do. Her horse slowly walked toward him. They both let out neighs.

Holden put his arm around her shoulders. "If we leave them alone, I think they'll start to make friends."

She looked up at him. "Why didn't you tell me about all this?"

"Honestly, I've been so focused on finding your husband's killer, I've been in a different world."

"Tell me one thing. I know you went into law enforcement because it appealed to you, but how were you able to leave here?"

His eyes narrowed on her features. "I was in so much

pain after losing Cynthia, I went into a depression. My parents felt I needed to get away in order to throw it off. At first I resented them for saying anything, but in time I knew they were right. Much as I hated leaving the family because I'm a rancher at heart, I realized I had to get away before nothing mattered anymore."

"I wanted to get away, too," she confessed. "But I couldn't do that to my little three-year-old boy."

"You had Chase to give you the will to go on living. I needed something, too. Being police chief and then sheriff in Whitebark meant new friends and surroundings. Right from the start I liked it there without all the old reminders.

"Then one amazing night, this beautiful blond woman in jeopardy came to my office. You know the rest. I fell head over heels in love and haven't been the same since."

"Neither have I."

He lowered his head and they kissed passionately while the horses wandered around getting used to each other.

Holden finally let her go. "We'll take them for a ride later and put them in the barn. Right now I'm dying for my parents to meet you."

"I want to get to know the people who raised you. I'd like to tell them what a perfect man you turned out to be."

His half smile caught at her heart. "Perfect? If you only knew. After my sisters and their families come over and we've eaten, we'll sit down and do some planning with the folks."

By the time they started walking toward the house,

his parents had come outside. They were talking to Chase who was still perched on the fencing.

Both were tall and good-looking. His mother had given him those luminous gray eyes. Mr. Granger had bequeathed Holden his build and hair color. His brown hair showed a few streaks of silver, making him very distinguished. She could already imagine how Holden would look when he got older.

Her chatty son had engaged them. "Holden knew where to find that yellow-bellied marmot. We fed it a doughnut and he ate it."

Everyone chuckled. Holden's mom turned to Jessica. "Congratulations on your engagement." She studied her for a moment before hugging her. "You poor darling for having to go through this ordeal," she said in a quiet voice. "We're so happy you'll stay with us for a few days. My son is a different man. It's all because of you."

"He's changed my whole life, too. Thank you for welcoming us to your home. It was completely Holden's idea."

"I know it was. We couldn't wait for you to come. Our son is terribly in love with you and is crazy about Chase. Those he loves, he cherishes."

"You're even more beautiful than the pictures Holden sent," his father said. "Welcome to the ranch. After what you've lived through, we hope you'll forget all the pain and worry and just enjoy being here."

"We already have."

He gave her a warm hug.

When she stepped away, he hunkered down by Chase. "The grandchildren are excited to know you've come. They're going to be jealous of that sheriff's hat you're wearing."

"Holden gave it to me. I love him. He's going to be my new dad."

Tears filled the older man's eyes.

Holden picked him up in his arms. "I love him and his mother. I love his nana, too. Come on, everyone. Let's go in the house. I'll show you where you're going to sleep." Mr. Granger went with them.

"Is it upstairs?"

"Yup. It's my old room. You can see for miles and miles from the window."

"Yay!"

Holden's mother smiled at Jessica. "They look so perfect together. It's as if they've known each other all their lives."

Jessica nodded. "That's how it felt from the moment we met. But before we do anything else, I want you to know something important about me before Holden says anything. I can't have any more children. The doctor told me I went through early menopause. I've talked all this over with Holden because I wanted him to meet someone else with whom he could have a baby."

"But he wouldn't hear of it," his mother broke in on her. "I can only understand how heartbroken you must have been to be given news like that, but it's clear he's deeply in love with you and hasn't let that matter."

"The trouble is, he'd make the most wonderful father."

His mother smiled through her tears. "You're right, but anyone can see that your adorable Chase already fills his life with joy. Thank you for telling me. I'm glad I know and can tell the rest of the family.

"When they find out, no one will ask any questions about that. Why don't we go inside and get you settled? The children will be over any minute now. They all adore their uncle Holden."

Jessica smiled. "I adore him, too. So much it hurts."

"I can relate," his mother said. "That's how I feel about my husband."

"Thanks again for making us all feel so welcome."

"We want to do whatever we can. We're so happy Holden brought you here now. It will be easier for all of us to plan a wedding date that suits everyone. Does your mother have some dates in mind?"

"She's waiting to hear dates from you."

Holden's mother was wonderful.

Within a half hour the rest of the family had driven over and everyone got acquainted while they ate a delicious meal. Jessica liked his family a lot. Chase was going to have two cousins plus another cousin who would be born in a few months. Having to share their uncle was a little hard for Rob and Chrissy. Jessica could tell she was used to Holden's attention and a little jealous of his interest in Chase. Jessica talked to Holden about it later when they said good-night before going to separate bedrooms.

"Give them time and they'll work it out."

"I know they will."

He kissed her long and hard. "See you in the morning. We'll go riding while he plays with his cousins."

It was torture letting Holden go, but Jessica had to remember this wouldn't go on for too much longer.

The next morning after they'd had breakfast, they rode out on the Granger ranch and talked about the future. When they reached a spot near a small lake, they dismounted.

Holden pulled a blanket out of his saddlebag and threw it on the grass. Then he pulled her down next to him. For the next hour they lost themselves in each other until he tore his lips from hers and got to his feet.

"We'd better go, or the honeymoon will start right here. I want you to be my wife first."

Holden was such an honorable man. She adored him for it and stood up. This time she folded the blanket and put it in the saddlebag so he didn't have to use his injured hand.

They headed back to the ranch house and talked about her career. "I'll keep working at the beauty salon, but I don't think Mom is going to hold on to it much longer."

"Why do you say that?"

"I think there's going to be another wedding in the not too distant future. I told you she's been seeing a man named Ray Marsden from the church. He's a rancher who lost his wife, and she's crazy about him. He wants to marry her and take her traveling, but we'll see."

"Do you think you might want to teach school and get your degree? You know I'll support you in anything you'd like to do."

"I do know, and maybe I will, but right now all I can think about is being a wife to you. What about you? You said you were a rancher at heart."

"I've been thinking about that."

Just to hear him say that got her excited. "I'll bet you have. As I told you yesterday, after coming here I don't see how you ever gave this up."

He eyed her steadily. "How would you feel if we moved here and built our own ranch house on my property in a few years?"

"If it's what you really want deep down, then I want it for us."

"Let me think about it. It could be hard on Chase."

"Only because he would have to leave his nana. But she would come and visit us often, and we'd go there to visit Joey.

"So the decision of where we live and what you want to do for the rest of your life is up to you, darling. All I can say is, if you resign as sheriff one of these days, Whitebark will never find another sheriff who can hold a candle to you."

She heard him take a deep breath. "What star was I born under to meet a woman like you?"

Tears filled her eyes. "I'm still trying to believe you've asked me to marry you. I love you so much."

"Let's get back to Chase and talk to him."

Jessica loved it that he was so concerned for her son and his feelings.

When they reached the ranch house, all three children ran up to them outside the barn. Just as Holden had predicted, it appeared they'd become good friends.

"Mom, guess what? Baby follows us around and lets us feed her apple slices. I think she really likes me, Holden."

"Of course she does." He laughed in pure happiness. "She's like a baby and loves the attention. What else have you been doing?"

"We played out in the yard on the waterslide and got to help Grandma Granger make lemonade."

Grandma Granger already. Jessica smiled to see how fast the bond had happened.

"She let us sell it outside."

"Did lots of people buy it?"

Chrissy nodded. "Mom, Grandpa, Uncle Joe and Benny."

"He takes care of the horses," Chase explained, causing Holden's smile to turn into a grin.

"And Mike," Chrissy added. "He mows the lawn."

"Mike let us ride around with him." This from Chase.

Jessica laughed. "I bet that was a blast."

"I loved it!"

They rode into the barn and dismounted. The children followed them. "How much money did you make for mowing?" Holden wanted to know.

"We each got six quarters."

"What are you going to spend it on?"

"Grandpa said we should save our money."

"That sounds like my father."

"Can I spend any of it?"

"Of course. You earned it."

"How soon do we have to go back to Whitebark?" Holden glanced at Jessica. "Tomorrow."

"Do you have to go to work?"

"For just a little while."

"Heck."

"We'll come back soon."

"Come on, Chase. Grandma says it's time to go in and wash our hands. We're going to have dinner pretty soon."

"Okay. See you in a minute, Mom."

When they ran off, Holden put his arm around Jessica. "On our way home tomorrow we'll put the question to Chase and see how he feels."

The next morning, they loaded the horses in the trailer after hugging everyone goodbye.

"I wish we didn't have to go home yet."

Jessica smiled. That son of hers wished his life away. "We had a wonderful time, didn't we?"

"Yeah. Rob and Chrissy didn't want me to leave."

"I can see why," Holden responded. "Let me ask you something," he said when they were out on the highway. "After your mom and I are married, what would you think if we moved to Cody?"

"But how could you? You're the sheriff!"

"That's true, but what if I gave that up and started ranching again?"

"But where would we live?"

"We'll build a ranch house on my property adjoining my parents' with a barn and a corral."

Chase was quiet for so long, Jessica knew he was having a struggle. "Would Nana come with us?"

Jessica knew that was on his mind. "She'd come to visit often and we'd go see her."

"Don't you like being sheriff?" Chase asked Holden.

"I like it very much. It's how I met your mom."

"But would you rather be a rancher?"

"I'm happy doing both."

Except that Jessica knew how he really felt. Though he'd been a police officer, he would have eventually become a full-time rancher if his wife hadn't died.

"I want to know how *you* feel about it. Think about it, and when you know what matters most to you, tell me."

"I don't need to think about it."

"How come?"

"Every night I pray that you won't get killed by a bad guy. If you're a rancher, you'll be safe, so I'd rather we moved to Cody."

In Jessica's heart, she knew what his answer meant to Holden. It was an answer to her prayers, too. When he glanced at her, his eyes shone like molten silver.

Chapter 13

Two weeks after the wedding invitations had gone out, Holden phoned Jessica from his office. "I just got a call from Porter that the guys are throwing me a bachelor party tonight at Angelino's. I may be late getting to your house."

"Hmm. I wonder what that's going to be like."

"I'll let you know."

"If you dare."

He grinned and left headquarters to meet with them.

Holden couldn't help but be touched by the outpouring of best wishes and congratulations from his friends after he arrived. So many guys dropped in throughout the evening from both the fire and police departments. They included Chief Wayland, Chief Powell and Norm Selkirk, head of Sublette County Law Enforcement who'd been the person who'd suggested Holden should run for sheriff.

To his surprise even Commissioner Rich, the head of the Arson Task Force, and Arnie Blunt from the Wyoming State Fire Services Department showed up. They'd all worked together on other cases, one in particular when an arsonist lighting ranches on fire was finally caught by Cole, who'd figured out what was going on.

Wyatt led them in a toast after they'd enjoyed an Italian dinner. "I guess I don't have to tell everyone that the eligible females of Sublette County are going to go into mourning when they hear the sheriff is no longer available. I'm only thankful that my wife—before she became my wife—got stuck in a snowstorm on the mountain with me and the sheep before she met him."

"You're full of it," Holden called out as the guys hooted and hollered.

Cole got to his feet. "You've been the topic of conversation with my wife and sister-in-law on more than one occasion since you moved to Whitebark, Holden. They know you and I are friends and they've wanted to hear all the gossip they could about you. Frankly, I'm glad you're marrying Jessica so they'll stop pestering me for information."

The room roared with laughter.

When Cole sat down, Porter got up. "I guess I'm the only one here who's sorry to see you bite the dust. You were my last buddy to hang out with who didn't have to go home to anyone."

Holden chuckled. "We'll still hang out, Porter. We all will."

"I'm going to hold you to that." Porter lifted his glass. "Here's to you and Jessica and her cute little guy, Chase."

After more toasts from the group, the evening came

to an end. The close camaraderie between them made it an unforgettable night. When he left the party, Holden had to go to the office and leave a final list of instructions for Walt. He would be acting as undersheriff in Holden's absence because tomorrow Holden was getting married and would be taking five whole days off.

The smell of gardenias filled the lovely church in Whitebark. Jessica, wearing a white lace gown and matching veil, stood in the foyer holding a sheaf of gardenias and white roses in her left arm.

She could hear the organ music. The 11:00 a.m. ceremony was about to start. Chase smiled up at her with a sweet expression that lit his face and eyes. He looked so adorable in his tux, her heart melted. Since her father couldn't do the honors, she wanted her son at her side. He was also going to be the ring bearer and had put the rings in his jacket pocket.

"Are you ready, honey?"

"Yup."

She grasped his hand in hers and they began the walk down the aisle past a full congregation of friends and family. Donna and Lily sat with Wilma and Joey. Their children waved to Chase. He waved back. It was so cute. Millie and her husband sat behind them.

When they neared the front, they passed Jessica's mother who sat with Ray and her church friends on one side of the aisle.

Holden's family sat on the other side, Rob and Chrissy with their parents. Chrissy sat closest to the aisle. She let her arm dangle over the pew and waved it slowly back and forth, like she was teasing a kitty.

The action was so funny, Jessica struggled not to

laugh out loud. She thought Chase might laugh, too, but he managed to hold on to his dignity.

Holden, who stood next to his father, had been watching her out of those silvery eyes from his stance near the pastor. She could hardly breathe when their gazes collided. As her mother had said earlier, Holden looked so splendid in his tux, no one would notice anyone else.

She was right. Jessica was so in love with her handsome hero, she'd been functioning in a daze. When she reached him, Chase handed her bouquet to Jessica's mother, then he walked around to stand on Holden's other side while his father sat down.

The pastor smiled at the three of them.

"Isn't this a blessed sight? Today is truly a glorious day the Lord hath made. Today both of you are blessed with God's greatest of all gifts—the gift of abiding love. All those present here wish both of you all the joy, happiness and success the world has to offer.

"As you travel through life together, I caution you to remember that the true measure of joy and peace is to be found within the love you hold in your hearts. Hold that key to your hearts very tightly.

"Now if you will please face each other and repeat after me."

Finally, they were saying the vows that she had been imagining for so long.

"Since Holden and Jessica have pledged to love each other forever, I now pronounce them man and wife. Holden? Do you have a ring for your bride?"

"I do." He turned to Chase, who put it in his hand. The two smiled at each other before he faced Jessica and slid it home.

"Jessica? Do you have a ring for your husband?"

"Yes."

Chase walked around and handed it to her. She gave him a kiss, then turned to Holden. He put out his left hand and she slid the gold band that she'd bought in Cody on his finger.

"You may now kiss your bride."

"Jessica," Holden whispered before kissing her such a long time it brought heat to her face. The organist started to play the wedding march. After Holden remembered where they were, he put his arm around her waist and they walked down the aisle past their beaming parents.

Chase followed them outside where they were besieged by everyone wanting to congratulate them. Before long, they were driven in Holden's father's car to the Whitebark Hotel for the reception. Holden kissed her all the way there.

A huge party, as Chase called it, awaited them in the main ballroom. Though Jessica loved it, she kept thinking about the time when they were going to be alone. They'd been apart too long and she was eager to have Holden all to herself.

They'd planned to spend their wedding night at the hotel, then go back to her house. Jessica knew this would be hard on Chase whose Nana would be taking care of him overnight. Holden promised to take her on a honeymoon in a few months.

Before they left for their room, Jessica took Chase upstairs. "Do you know how proud I am of you? Everyone tells me I have the most wonderful son in the whole world. But guess what? I've already known that from the day you were born."

He was trying to be brave. "How long are you going to be gone?"

"We'll be back tomorrow and Nana will bring you to the house."

Chase blinked. "I thought you'd be gone longer."

"No."

The relief on his face spoke volumes. She and Holden had talked it over. This was a new situation for Chase to adjust to. He needed time. "I love you, honey." She hugged and kissed him.

Just then Holden walked in on them. He looked so amazing in his tux, it took her breath away.

"Everyone says I'm the luckiest man in the world to be married to your mom and have a boy like you to love. You mean the world to me, Chase."

"I love you, too."

"Come here and give me a hug. We'll be back tomorrow."

"That's what mom says."

"Yup. And when you get to the house, we'll go to a movie and then the Spaghetti Factory."

"When will Nana bring me?"

Holden flashed her a help message. Jessica had to think fast. "We should be home by two o'clock." She could read Holden's mind. They had sixteen hours from now until then.

"Yay!" He ran into Holden's arms.

Jessica's mother walked in the hotel bedroom. Jessica hugged her mom. "Thank you for everything."

"I believe this is the happiest day of my life. To see you and Chase this happy means everything."

"I want you to be happy, too, Mom. We're going

to talk about you and Ray before long. It's time you started thinking about your own future."

She blushed. "One wedding at a time."

"You know what I mean. You've had full responsibility of me for the past two years. It's time you did all the things you've wanted to do with Ray. I'm aware of all the sacrifices you've made for me. You've always been so busy helping me, he can hardly get time in with you. We're going to fix that!" She gave her a kiss.

"See you tomorrow, honey."

Holden opened the door to their hotel room and carried Jessica across the threshold. Shoving it closed with his foot, he carried her through the foyer to the bed and followed her down with his body.

"I've been dreaming of this moment for so long, I've come close to losing my mind. These weeks of waiting have been pure torture. When you came down the aisle in your wedding dress, I felt like I'd been struck by a bolt of lightning. This gorgeous, fabulous woman was actually going to marry me. Jessica—make love to me, darling?"

"You never have to ask me that. I've been yours from the beginning and you know it. I need you so badly, I can't think straight anymore."

Her mouth clung to his, exulting in the passion he aroused in her. Being loved by him was ecstasy beyond comprehension. Nothing else registered but the joy of showing him what he meant to her. Throughout the rest of the day and night, she sought only to bring him pleasure.

Jessica was thankful she'd been born a woman. His touch sent her into rapture and made her feel immortal. Holden was such a beautiful man. She adored him and couldn't stop telling him how much she loved him.

In the middle of the night he rolled her over on top of him. She found she was as insatiable as her husband. Jessica not only had a husband, she had the most wonderful lover on earth. Every time he touched her she experienced indescribable delight and never wanted it to end.

At one point they both fell asleep. When she opened her eyes later, loving it that their legs were entwined, she couldn't bear it that he wasn't awake. His left arm lay across her hip.

She carefully lifted his hand where the doctor had splinted his baby finger. To think a bullet had grazed it enough to cause a fracture made her realize more than ever how precious his life was to her. He'd fought for her and had slain a dragon.

Jessica pressed her lips to the back of his hand, loving him so deeply it actually caused a pain in her heart. How, out of all the women he'd ever known, had she been lucky enough to win his love? He was a unique man with a mixture of abilities and talents.

Any woman lucky enough to be his wife needed to be understanding of him. She was married to a sheriff. Every day that he left for work, he put his life on the line. Every night that she expected him to come back to her, he might be late or might not come home at all. That was the risk she'd chosen to take marrying him because life with him was worth everything, no matter how long or short that time would be.

But maybe that was going to change. Chase had said he was willing to move to Cody, but it was still a big decision for Holden. She'd have to wait and see.

"Darling?"

At the sound of his deep voice, she lifted her head.

"Why the tears?" He was alarmed. "Why are you crying?"

Jessica kissed him for a long time, not allowing him to talk.

"Don't mind me. I'm so terribly in love with you that I can't believe I'm your wife. You're this amazing man who has committed your life to serve other people, yet you're in constant danger. Do you have any idea how much I admire you? I guess if I've been crying it's because I've been counting my blessings."

"I've been doing that since the day I met you. I just keep wondering how I can be deserving of your love."

"Holden, stop talking about being deserving."

"You're right. We just have to accept the fact that we're the luckiest married couple in the world with the sweetest boy alive. He won over everyone's hearts at the church. That's because you're an exceptional mother and it shows. Chrissy is already nuts about him and that isn't easy to accomplish."

"You couldn't see her from where you were standing." Jessica told him about the way she dangled her arm before waving at Chase.

That deep, rich laughter she loved broke out of him. "I loved our wedding, but I didn't eat enough food because I was too excited to get you alone. I'll call for room service, then I need to make love to you all over again until we have to leave for the ranch. Don't move."

She lay still while he ordered their breakfast. While they waited for it to arrive, she traced the outline of his features with her finger. Soon there was a knock on the door.

He kissed her lips and grabbed a towel to hitch around his hips. "Be right back."

She sat up in the bed. "Please hurry. I can't live without you."

"Mrs. Granger? This is just the beginning."

Epilogue

By New Year's, their new five-bedroom ranch house had been built in Cody. The moving van came from Whitebark. Little by little, with the Grangers' help, they started to make it into their home.

Chase was ecstatic with his new bedroom upstairs that had a window seat so he could look out over a white landscape and the Absaroka Mountains. He and Chrissy ran up and down the stairs all day long having the time of their lives.

Chase's nana had come to help. Jessica was thankful to be with her mom. Since Christmas, Jessica hadn't felt well and didn't know why. At first she'd attributed her fatigue to the move. But when she started to have periods of nausea, it worried her.

Her mother thought she must have the flu and insisted she see a doctor. Jessica didn't want to tell

Holden until she knew what was wrong. After telling him she and her mom were going into town to look for some new lamps, they left Chase with him and drove to an Instacare.

There was quite a lineup and she had to wait for her turn. Once she was shown into the doctor's office, she explained her symptoms.

The doctor checked her vital signs and temperature. "You seem to be in excellent health, Mrs. Granger. Perhaps you're coming down with the flu, but you're not running a fever. Have you considered that you might be pregnant?"

She shook her head. "I couldn't be. I was diagnosed with early menopause years ago."

He cocked his head. "That condition isn't always permanent."

"That's what my specialist told me, but he said it would be a miracle if I conceived again."

He smiled. "Do you believe in miracles?"

"Yes. When my husband proposed to me, *that* was a miracle."

"Let's do a urine test, just to rule it out."

"I'm afraid it will be a waste of time."

"Humor me."

"All right."

"The restroom is through there. You'll find a cup. Set it on the shelf when you're through. Then come back in here."

"All right." She knew the drill and had been through it many times while being married to Trent.

In a few minutes, she'd returned to his office and waited. Ten more minutes went by before he came in and shut the door behind him. "Sorry to keep you waiting. I just got your results. You're pregnant, Mrs. Granger."

Jessica almost fainted. "Are you positive?"

"Yes. I could do more tests, but I suggest you call your OB."

"I—I don't have one here," she stammered. "We just moved from Whitebark."

"Well, you need to get one right away. If you never expected to get pregnant, then you don't know how long you've been pregnant. You need prenatal care."

She got to her feet. "I can't believe this has happened."

"Is it good or bad news for you?"

Jessica took a deep breath. "It's the most wonderful news you could possibly imagine. Thank you, Doctor."

She flew out of the room and down the hall to the reception room. "Mom? We've got to get back to the ranch immediately."

They hurried out to the car. Her mom got behind the wheel. "What's wrong, honey?"

"You're going to be a grandmother again, but I have no idea when."

"Jessica!"

"He wanted to do a simple test. I told him it was pointless, but he insisted."

"Hooray for a thorough doctor."

"Hooray for miracles, Mom."

Tears streamed down her cheeks as they drove through the snow to her new ranch house. She got out of the car and ran in the house.

"Holden?" she cried.

"I'm in the den setting up the computer."

She flew through the living room and down the hall. He met her in the doorway. "What's wrong?"

"Are you ready for the most amazing, wonderful news of your life?"

Jessica could hear his mind working. "There's only one piece of news that would qualify on that level."

She nodded. "That's it."

"We're pregnant."

"Yes! I just came from the doctor."

Her husband had lived through many death-defying experiences in his life and had handled them with strength and heroism. But this one was different. She thought he was going to collapse.

"Sit down, darling."

He did her bidding. Jessica crawled onto his lap and put her arms around his neck. She kissed every inch of his rugged features. "I'm convinced our love was meant to be, my beloved husband. Now you're going to know the joy of watching your own baby come into the world."

"Mom?"

She turned as Chase came in the den. "Hi, honey. Guess what?"

"What?" He had a concerned look on his face.

"Holden and I are going to have a baby."

"A baby?"

"Yup." Holden finally found his voice.

"A boy or a girl?"

"We don't know yet," he answered, obviously starting to believe it.

Jessica slid off his lap and walked over to her son. "Think how fun this is going to be for you. A little brother or sister who doesn't know anything. You'll have to teach him or her everything! They'll be the luckiest baby in the world to have a big brother like you. I never had one and wished I did."

He looked up at her in astonishment. "When's it going to come?"

"Maybe by summer."

"Where's it going to sleep?"

"Which bedroom shall we turn into a nursery? We'll let you decide."

"I'll go look."

As he dashed out of the den, she felt Holden's arms wrap around her from behind and felt his tears on her cheeks and neck. "Every dream of mine has just come true. If you only knew," he said in a broken voice.

"I know. From the moment I met you, I lived with the pain that if I could ever get you to love me, I could never give you a child. Talk about a wonderful life."

"It's wonderful because you're in it. Never let me go, my love."

"As if I could." She turned in his arms. "Congratulations, Daddy."

* * * * *

Shania flushed as she raised her eyes toward Daniel. "I don't usually babble like this."

Daniel found the pink hue that had suddenly risen to her cheeks rather sweet. The next second, he realized that he was staring. Daniel forced himself to look away. "I hadn't noticed."

"Yes, you had," Shania contradicted. "But I think that it's very nice of you to pretend that you hadn't." When she heard Daniel laugh softly to himself, she asked him, "What's so funny?" before she could think to stop herself.

"I'm not accustomed to hearing the word *nice* used to describe me," he admitted.

Didn't the man have any close friends? Someone to bolster him up when he was down on himself? "You're kidding."

The lopsided smile answered her before he did. "Something else I'm not known for."

She pretended that he was a student and she did a quick assessment of the man before her. "You know you're being very hard on yourself."

"Not hard," he contradicted. "Just honest."

She had no intention of letting this slide. If he had been one of her students, she would have done what she could to raise his spirits—or maybe it was his self-esteem that needed help.

"Well, I think you're nice—and you do have a sense of humor."

"If you say so," Daniel replied, not about to dispute the matter. He had a feeling that arguing with Shania would be pointless. "But just so you know, I'm not about to chuck my career and become a stand-up comedian."

She grinned at his words. "See, I told you that you had a sense of humor," she declared happily.

Don't miss
The Lawman's Romance Lesson *by Marie Ferrarella,*
available April 2019 wherever
Harlequin® Special Edition books and ebooks are sold.

www.Harlequin.com

HSEEXP0319

Looking for more satisfying love stories
with community and family at their core?

**Check out Harlequin® Special Edition
and Love Inspired® books!**

New books available every month!

CONNECT WITH US AT:

Facebook.com/groups/HarlequinConnection

 Facebook.com/HarlequinBooks

 Twitter.com/HarlequinBooks

 Instagram.com/HarlequinBooks

 Pinterest.com/HarlequinBooks

ReaderService.com

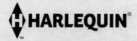

**ROMANCE WHEN
YOU NEED IT**

HFGENRE2018

Hannah exhaled. "My point is that you should consider doing the 100-Day Mustang Challenge."

Tripp looked her up and down. The woman was a sassy thing for a stranger who'd only arrived a few days ago.

"You don't even know if you'll be here in one hundred days," he returned.

Though her eyes said she·was dumbstruck by his bold statement, her mouth kept moving. "You don't believe I'm related to the Maxwells, do you?"

Tripp raised both hands. "I don't know what to believe." Though he tried not to judge, there was a part of him that had already stamped the woman's card and dismissed her.

"I am, and I'm willing to stick around to find out if it will help Clementine."

"Help Clementine?"

Hannah offered a shrug "We could use a little nest egg to start over."

"The prize money?"

"Sure. Why not? If I make it possible for you to train, maybe it would be worth some of the purse." The flush of her cheeks told him that her words were all bravado.

"What makes you think I'm going to win?" Tripp asked.

"I've seen you with the horses." She paused. "I know a winner when I see one."

He nearly laughed aloud. "So what kind of split are we talking about here?" he asked.

"Fifty-fifty."

Tripp released a scoffing sound. "In your dreams, lady. I'm the trainer and I'm paying for fees and feed and everything else out of my pocket."

"Sixty-forty?"

"More like seventy-thirty, and you have a deal." The words slipped from his mouth before he could take them back. What was he thinking, making a pact with a pregnant single mother who might very well prove to be a seasoned con artist? His mouth hadn't run off on him in years. Yet here he was, with his good sense galloping away.

"I, um…"

Despite his misstep, Hannah seemed reluctant to commit, and that stuck in his craw. Was she having second thoughts about his ability to win the challenge?

"What's the problem?" he asked. "Your bravado seems to be fading the closer it gets to the chute."

"Seventy-thirty?" She shook her head in disagreement.

"Are you telling me that you couldn't start over with fifteen thousand dollars? If you can't, then you're doing it all wrong, my friend."

"We aren't friends," Hannah said. Then she stood and walked over to his desk. She offered him her hand, and he stared at it for a moment before accepting the handshake.

"Deal," she said.

Tripp stared at her small hand in his.

The day had started off like any other. In a heartbeat, everything was sideways.

Don't miss
Her Last Chance Cowboy *by Tina Radcliffe,*
available March 2019 wherever
Love Inspired® *books and ebooks are sold.*

www.LoveInspired.com

Love Harlequin romance?

DISCOVER.

Be the first to find out about promotions, news and exclusive content!

Facebook.com/HarlequinBooks

Twitter.com/HarlequinBooks

Instagram.com/HarlequinBooks

Pinterest.com/HarlequinBooks

ReaderService.com

EXPLORE.

Sign up for the Harlequin e-newsletter and download a free book from any series at **TryHarlequin.com.**

CONNECT.

Join our Harlequin community to share your thoughts and connect with other romance readers!
Facebook.com/groups/HarlequinConnection

HARLEQUIN®

**ROMANCE WHEN
YOU NEED IT**

HSOCIAL2018